What people are saying about "Lusting For Love"

"Lusting For Love is the perfect parallel to the realistic views and experiences of modern day romance. The author creates a visual journey into the lives of her multiple characters, and takes you on an emotional, and intriguing exploration."
Kaidy-Ann Ellis- Advanced Reader

Definitely watch for upcoming novels by this author. McDonald is expected to deliver!

"Lusting For Love" will satisfy readers and have them yearning for more. It captures the ups and downs of new relationships while staying true to the realities of life, dating, friendship, and personal battles. Don't be surprised when talented first time writer McDonald delivers in future novels."
Kerwin Pilgrim - AMLS, Brooklyn Public Library

Lusting For Love

(a novel)

by

Nicola McDonald

Nicola McDonald

NewN Publishing
PO Box 1307
Bronx NY 10462

This book is a work of fiction. Names, characters, places and incidents are either products of the author's imagination or are used fictitiously. Any resemblance to actual events, locales, or persons, living or dead, is entirely coincidental.

Lusting For Love. Copyrighted © 2004 by Nicola McDonald. All rights reserved. No part of this book may be used or reproduced in any manner whatsoever without permission except in the case of brief quotations embodied in critical articles and reviews.

Direct all information requests to NewN Publishing. PO Box 1307, Bronx NY 10462.
For information regarding special discounts on bulk purchases please contact NewN Publishing at n_mcd@newnpublishing.com or fax requests to 718-792-3066

www.newnpublishing.com

Publisher's Cataloging-in-Publication
(Provided by Quality Books, Inc.)

McDonald, Nicola (Nicola L.)
 Lusting for love : a novel / by Nicola McDonald.
 p. cm.
 LCCN 2004107042
 ISBN 0-9753950-0-9

 1. Man-woman relationships--Fiction. 2. Promiscuity--Fiction. 3. Deception--Fiction. 4. Love stories, American. I. Title.

PS3613.C3876L87 2004   813'.6
                    QBI04-700238

For Nearcisse and Nikayla Maynard

I love you both with all that I am.

Celine

It was not the long line to use the lavatory that really bothered me. However, it was the fact that I hopped from foot to foot trying to hold back nature while I waited hopelessly. No one even looked my way, much more to even think to offer up their turn. In fact, I thought I saw an older lady pout her lips, cut her eyes at me and toss her head. Anyway, I finally got a chance to relieve myself, which caused a big load to be lifted from my pelvis. I washed my hands and walked out enjoying my mellow mood.

"Ouch!" I yelled.

I did not mean to scare or blame him, it was just my natural reflexes.

"Oh Shit! I didn't see you coming," he countered.

He bent down and picked up the large bag of m & ms that fell from his hand. I watched as he stood again. Our eyes met and for an instant my thoughts were in total chaos. He was so beautiful, and yes definitely like a female. His brown eyes were so big and pretty surrounded by all those thick, luscious lashes. He had a nice russet complexion that beamed its smoothness. The thick braids that crowned his head made him look to be of Indian descent, which made him look even sexier to me. I was never so affected at first sight by any man before; I wanted to devour him right then.

"Oh, I'm sorry. It's oklay, I...I mean it's okay I am partly at fault also," I stammered.

I do not know where he found the courage, but I was glad when he stuck out his hand, looked deep into my eyes and said... he said, " hi my name is Chris."

I took the softness of his palm in a hand lock, "Celine, nice to meet you."

We spoke about so much in those few minutes that it felt as though I had known the man for so much longer. Something about his presence had me mesmerized. Still, my sudden attraction held me in disbelief because it was highly unlikely of me to become acquainted with anyone, especially so fast. I was always enlightened about my clear-cut 'beware' facial attitude that stuck to my whole body expressions.

My intention to call my best friend Sheria had quickly subsided when I imagined what she would have been doing. So that night I had gone to the movies alone to watch the latest movie out. I had been home bored and figured that a movie was my best bet. Therefore, when Chris suggested that I sit with him and his friends I went along.

Chris whispered small phrases to me every now and then, and even asked if I was fine. I liked that he was so concerned although we had only met an hour earlier. After the movie was done Chris's friends left because they drove separately. We spoke for a little while in a close-by diner. Although I really did not want to leave, we parted with hopes and unspoken promises of seeing each other again and perhaps creating something much more. I went home with a totally different frame of mind and dreamed about him with butterflies in the pit of my stomach. I knew that I so wanted to see him again.

I awoke the next morning with glee and anticipation that Chris would call to ask me out. But when he did not call by noon, I retired to my routine Sunday afternoon escapades. I called up my parents to say "hi," did some yoga and then took an afternoon nap.

When I got up at about four in the afternoon I went for a stroll in the park. As usual, I stopped in my favorite ice-cream store and ordered a double scooped chocolate strawberry cone.

"Hi Celine," Paps greeted as I asked him to serve me my usual.

"Hey Paps! How are you today?"

"Fine chile, just fine."

He was a gray-haired black man seemingly in his late fifties and from the South by his accent. One thing I liked about his place was that he knew how to serve his customers well; he was very polite and friendly.

"Thank you and enjoy the rest of your day," I said while gladly accepting my ice cream.

"Same to you dear, same to you," he replied as I walked out the door licking my lips.

In the park I sat on a bench close to the playground. This park was so huge. Therefore, people could have actually gotten lost in it if they strayed enough. However, I always went to the same spot so there were no such misfortunes for me. The weather was about seventy degrees out and a little on the windy side, and that made the temperature not too hot just good enough. There were little kids swinging, one of the little girls wore a red dress with a red and white pair of sneakers and laughed hysterically while her mom pushed her. Two other girls who looked to be about ten and eight years old chased each other around throwing a ball. I admired their energy even as I wondered when my chance would come that I might love a tiny human so unconditionally. I walked passed them and went to sit on a bench not far away.

I liked strolling around occasionally because sweet air in the atmosphere made me feel so much at ease. I loved to admire the different colors of trees and how people from different backgrounds fitted in the environment. I sat, continued to devour my ice cream and listened to the variety of sounds that filled the air. My diaphragm contracted and relaxed as oxygen filled my lungs, which then released carbon dioxide.

    I positioned myself more comfortably on the wooden bench that had recently been repainted a lighter brown shade. I leaned back and closed my eyes then Chris's face popped up in my view. My lips voluntarily curled upwards as I visualized his silky skin tone and his mesmerizing eyes. It was still hard to accept the huge effects that he had on me. I wondered to myself what all that meant. My lips curled upwards again as I fixed a more detailed picture of Chris in my mind. I definitely had fun the night before and was hoping that he would call soon.

Chris

There was radiance in her whole spirit and indescribable warmth that came from her hazel eyes when she looked at me. When we met on Saturday I had every intention of calling Celine. She seemed like a delightful person to be around. Yet, I did not really want to show all that so soon and so I had decided to wait. It was now Monday evening and I had waited until I thought she was home and already settled in. Celine picked up on the third ring sounding breathless.

"Hello," she answered.

"Hi Celine, it's Chris. How are you?"

"I'm fine, how are you doing?"

"I'm doing good. I'm calling to see if you have plans for this weekend. Maybe we can go catch a movie or do something else if you don't mind?"

I was feeling a little shaky inside just incase her reply was no.

"Sure, I don't have any plans. Do you like bowling?"

"Yeah, that's one of my hobbies," I responded.

"Great then. We can go to the bowling alley inside the Port Authority station in Manhattan, and then swing around the corner to the see a movie."

"That's fine with me. Say seven?"

"Sure, I'll call you later in the week to confirm."

"Ok then bye."

"Bye."

Her voice sounded so sexy that I could listen to her words all day long. It had been at least six months since

I last went on a date and so I was very excited about my plans with Celine.

My cell phone rang just then and snapped me out of daydream land.

"Hey, what's up Pete?"

"What's up son? You on your way to the gym yet? Today I'm gon' teach your ass what's up."

"Nah cuz, I didn't leave yet. But I wouldn't miss it for the world. You should know we'll be setting the record today when we whoop your ass for the third time straight," I said laughing.

Pete was on the other end laughing too.

"Whatever man. I'll catch you later."

"Aight."

Pete was my boy. It seemed like forever since we had known each other because over the years we had gotten so close. I could not even remember a time that I needed him and he was not there.

"Yeah!" I yelled as I jumped in the air.

We were close to the end of the game and there was no way that they could beat our leading forty-one to thirty-five score. Then the game started getting intense in the last couple minutes. Andrew from Pete's team had the ball bouncing towards our net. Suddenly, he was swiftly lifted from the ground as his arms stretched out letting go of a straight three-pointer into the net. Then, as if he inherited springs, Pete retrieved the ball mid-air, sprinted towards the net and scored a next three-pointer forcing us into overtime. During the first five minutes Pete's team scored two points that caused them to win.

"Yeah! That's what I'm talking 'bout," Pete yelled coming up to me for a pound.

"Aight man calm down," I replied, "Y'all got lucky this time around."

I was laughing while smacking fists with him.

"Oh come on you sore loser," he said knowing I was only teasing him.

"Ok son you win straight up. I've been teaching you well, huh?"

He laughed, "whateva man. I ain't even gonna go there."

"It was worth a try. Anyway, word up good game man."

By that time it was about seven thirty going on eight in the evening. So after some vocal celebration, I gave the group high fives and headed home.

Thoughts of Celine challenged my mind each time I was alone. That moment had been no different as I sped down the highway. I was boggled by my difficulty to understand how a woman I met less than forty-eight hours earlier had such striking effect on me. I welcomed the feeling, yet the beats that my heart danced to were too fast for me to keep up with. I steadied my mind and decided to see how things would roll out during our date to come.

Sheria

I gazed at myself in the mirror while I prepared to go out with Keron. I looked hot as usual, if I may say so myself. I was dressed in a pair of blue stone-washed jeans with a white tube top, and a pair of white two-inch strapless pumps. I heard the bell ring just as I finished applying my coral sand lipstick. I replaced the cover and placed it on my dresser while I rubbed my lips together. My eyes darted in the direction of my clock.

"Good I like when my men are punctual," I said to myself.

After one last look at my luscious self I wined my hips to get the door.

"Hi beau." I greeted.

While my eyes undressed and seduced him I slithered my tongue against the edges of my top teeth.

"Hey there yourself sexy," he said.

His naughty thoughts portrayed on his face and I knew instantly that the wait to bed him would have been tough.

"Are you ready for some fun?" I asked.

I was in the mood for long laughs and carelessness to an extent. It was a beautiful Thursday evening, and that was perfect because his class was in the evening and I was off that Friday. Although it probably would not have made a difference if I had to work.

We went to the Village and walked around for a while enjoying the scenery, then to an art museum not too far away. Our time spent together had been interesting, but my most yearned for part of the day was yet to come.

Keron and I were in his white Toyota Corolla on our way back home. He was amazingly sexy and funny, and I could hardly control myself. Sexiness in the form of a great sense of humor was such a huge turn-on for me, and at that moment turn-on was hardly the correct word. I felt my nipples harden and wetness soiled my panties. I tried to slow down the trickling by pressing my legs together, but all that did was worsen the situation by getting me more engorged. By the time we got to my apartment my panties swam in sweet juices.

"Would you like to come up for some dessert Keron?" I asked not trying to conceal the fact that I wanted to seduce him.

"Would love to, thought you'd never ask."

He parked the car and we walked a little stretch of a pavement to get to my studio. Keron sat on the couch and got comfortable as I went in the kitchen and got us both some pistachio-coconut flavored ice cream. I handed one cup to him and sat in a chair across the room facing his direction. I was unable to control my hormones any longer, which led to my assault of the spoon that I used to feed myself. Keron had a devious look on his face, but he was moving too damn slow for me. I was long ready to rip off his tan tee and short pants. I only needed enough access to the body parts that mattered to me the most. My straightforwardness surprised many people at times; still my motto remained 'why act when you know what you want'. And right about that time that thing sticking up in his pants was what I wanted. I lowered my tube top and exposed my huge chocolate breasts with pierced, hardened nipples. Then I dripped a bit of ice cream on each and licked them clean. The intensity of the coldness against my body got me more wet. I got up and went over to him. He grabbed my ass aggressively and devoured me right there on the ground.

Celine

Friday came after much anticipation, however, there was still a few hours ahead before our date. We had agreed that Chris would pick me up at seven that evening. The day before, after work I had gotten a head start by getting my hair done so there was not much for me to do.

I sat in my leather chair with my feet high on my desk. My mind led me outside of my office to a land that I enjoyed. I had been day dreaming about Chris excessively all week. The butterflies in my stomach made me aware of the seriousness of my puppy love. Therefore, I sat at work counting each minute, which did not seem to pass by fast enough. My desk clock displayed five minutes to three, and that meant that I had two more hours to go. I decided to call Sheria since two days had gone by since I last heard from her.

"Hello?" she answered.

Exhaustion was written all over her voice.

"Hi girl!" I said.

"Hey! What's up sis?"

"I've been fine. How about you?"

"I'm just here, you know. Stayed out late last night."

"Girl don't you ever get tired of hanging out so much?"

"You must be kidding me right?" she asked.

I could visualize the thunderous roll of her eyes, yet that did not stop me.

"No! And all those men you be hanging with..."

"Hey, I'm tired. Please don't give me a lecture right now."

The grouch in her tried to rear its ugly head, but I ignored her.

"Do you ever want to hear it?" I challenged.

Silence exploded from the next end, but I knew Sheria was still there probably fighting the urge to hang up on me.

"Alright I give up, go back and rest. Call me some time this week, ok? Love you."

"Love you too. I'll talk with you later," she gladly responded and hung up.

I knew Sheria well enough to know that she did not want the truth to be verbalized. Continuous attempts to get her to give up her ways of promiscuity proved to be useless. I supposed that eventually she would give it up on her own time. At least I hoped she would.

As soon as the clock ticked four fifty-five I bum-rushed the office exit and headed towards my car.

"Enjoy your weekend Ms. Perry."

The familiar voice came from the security guard at the parking lot.

"You too Mr. Jeff."

"You sure are in a rush today."

He paused as if he was waiting for a response, preferably a detailed explanation of what was happening in my life that I was so thrilled about. I thought that it was just mostly women that were extremely nosy, but he was surely one very nosy older man.

"Well, you be careful," he said after a while.

"I will," was my response as I continued running towards my car.

Everything was already organized so there was not much to do besides get ready. When I stepped into my two-bedroom abode twenty minutes earlier than usual, feelings of anxiety stirred in me. I plopped down on the couch in search of tranquility. My eyes gazed around my house and I felt a warm gush of proudness inside. I had chosen to have the house repainted to a soothing lavender with white base after I purchased it a year ago. At first, my reluctance about buying my own house held me back because I believed that it was a most difficult process not worth it.

"It's a good collateral to have and when kids come into the picture that will be one less worry," was one of their strong points.

Eventually, I listened to my parents and I must say it was definitely worth it. I was free to do whatever I wanted because that was my own little space.

I went passed the living room and dinner area, down a slender hallway, then turned into the bathroom to my left to relieve myself. Then I went back out and up the stairs to my special place of sleep. Determining that I had more than enough time, I decided to take a nap. However, I was unable to sleep because my brain worked overtime wondering how my date would turn out. The excitement made my stomach flutter and once again I could hardly wait to see Chris.

After laying down a while I felt a bit rejuvenated. I went to my closet and took out my outfit that hung waiting for me since the day before. I fixed my hair and glossed my lips after getting dressed. When the time read six fifty-five my eager legs led me downstairs. I sat in my beige settee and waited for the five minutes gap to pass. Five minutes then became ten and ten became fifteen.

Usually, I was not a very patient person, but I found that my yoga ritual made me better in that department. I double checked my ringer, even called Sheria and asked her to call me back to make sure my phones worked. The sad part was that they did work and the saddest part yet, was that I had been stood up. I thought about calling Chris but decided against it. Finally, I took off my shoes and gave up hope.

Chris

I arrived at Celine's apartment at seven o'clock on the dot. My mother's advice on punctuality always stayed with me over the years. My right index finger pushed the little white buzzer. A few seconds passed before she answered. She looked so edible wearing a pair of tight black hip pants, fitted spaghetti strapped red shirt with an arc in the center revealing her pierced belly button. But her shoes were missing in action, while her feet showed off her pedicured nails.

"Hi, you look gorgeous," I complimented.

"Thanks!" she said in a dry tone.

Celine stared at me as though I had done something wrong.

"Are you ready?" I asked.

"Was there a lot of traffic or something? What happened to you?"

"What are you talking about?" I asked.

Celine looked impatient and slightly annoyed.

"You're late," she exclaimed.

I looked at my silver watch and noted that the time was one minute passed seven. I stood in total dismay and I was sure that it showed in my facial expression.

"Didn't we agree for seven?" I questioned.

"Yeah. It's now going for eight."

Celine pointed to the decorative clock on her wall to prove her point. It read the same time that I carried perhaps just a minute off.

"Oh gosh! What time is it?" she asked.

She looked once more at the clock to her left and then her hand found her mouth and covered it.

"I'm so sorry...I got ready by the clock in my bedroom and it is set ahead of time."

"It's okay as long as you don't mind if I tease you about it in the future."

Celine's smile revealed barely noticeable dimples in her cheeks.

"I'm ready if you are," I said.

"One sec. let me grab my purse and slippers from over there."

"Ok."

We walked to my car and I opened the door for her. I was old fashioned in that sense and I wanted to show her all that I was about.

During the fifteen-minute drive we spoke mostly about past bowling experiences.

"My very first day of bowling I was horribly embarrassed. I lined up the ball just the way I saw everyone else doing, swung my hand forward while making a dash for it down the lane. The next thing I knew, I was flying towards the pins with the ball still attached to my hand. I made it half way down the center and was so humiliated. Then, I got up apparently too quickly and deepened my embarrassment even more because I fell right back on my gluteus maximus."

She laughed lightly from remembrance.

"Then it got only worse when I felt millions of eyes piercing through me, some laughing."

"So none of your friends helped you?" I asked.

"First they were frozen from surprise because they did not at all expect me to fly down the bowling lane. Then by the time I got over to them their eyes were hysteric with laughter, although they tried to keep it in. I forgave them eventually. Now when I look back I cannot blame them. It was really funny."

"I can imagine the way you felt. I have a few humiliating experiences myself."

"Well, one day you must share."

"I'm not so sure about that. Only if you promise to be a good sport."

"Sure."

Celine smirked devilishly to let me know that she would not. I parked and we went to buy our movie tickets before going to the bowling alley. We waited for about fifteen minutes before there was an available lane.

"I like the way aha, aha, I'm bowling aha, aha!"

This was Celine cutely taunting me. We were halfway into the game and she was leading by five points. I was too distracted by her suaveness to show her my skills so I just smiled and enjoyed the kid in her. Celine was such an amusing and amazing person to be around. I was unwilling to leave when the next few minutes passed and the game was over. However, I still felt content because our night together was not quite over yet. We shook hands and hugged in honor of good sportsmanship.

Neither of us was hungry because earlier while waiting for our lane we had eaten curly fries and shrimps with sodas. So since we still had a whole half of an hour before the movie began we decided to walk around and take in the Manhattan scenery. The weather was a perfect seventy-eight degrees and the streets were excessively crowded as usual.

"This place is so amazing. Each time I come out here I feel so alive, the atmosphere gives off such livelihood."

Her eyes sparkled as she spoke.

"I know, it's like a whole different world," I agreed.

There was one man selling diagrams of different sexual positions on a piece of paper for one dollar each.

Another bunch of mostly Asian men and women sat along the sidewalks drawing portraits of people. There were many hot dog carts. And sometimes the variety of odors was too much for the sense of smell. Sometimes it could even create a slight headache or shortness of breath, especially during the allergy seasons. Of course, the various clothing fashions of all the people walking around was always a sight to behold. Many were out of the norm. But then again these days one had to really think about what was normal because everything seemed like norm if not to one person, to another.

By nine fifty-five we were in the theater trying to locate a seat. Most of the seats were occupied, but luckily we spotted two adjoining ones in the middle row of an isle closer towards the back. We had to be quick though because a couple behind us almost tried to run us over trying to get to them first.

We both had laughed quite a bit throughout the movie. I had enjoyed our time together and from the excitement in her voice and the enthusiastic look on her face, I could tell that Celine really enjoyed being with me too. We walked slowly, hand in hand for fifteen minutes to get to my car, while we talked and joked some more.

Sheria

It was Friday, one of my best days of the week. I had two glorious days to relax before another challenging workweek began again. My promise to call Celine concentrated my mind once more and so I palmed the beige cordless phone from the night stand. I sat and thought about Celine's mothering tendencies that sometimes got me so annoyed. She and I were the closest of friends, even as close as two sisters could ever get. Perhaps that was the reason that I naturally found her to be so bothersome at times.

Celine was quite the opposite of me when it came to our sex lives. While I enjoyed exploring different things and people, she had to be in a continuous relationship before giving up the goods. I never bothered her about her ways of handling shit, yet she forever stayed on me about my sexual preferences. Don't get me wrong I do love her to death with a capital D. Still, at times I found her motherly behavior towards me to be overbearing.

I reversed my memory to the task at hand and dialed eleven digits, then waited for her to answer. Celine's voice came alive on the second ring.

"'Sup sis?"

"Hey! What are you up to?" I asked her.

"Was just about to give you a call. What are you doing?"

"Calling you."

Laughter exploded from my lips thanks to my slick answer while she cracked up on the next side also.

"I know you're calling me miss slick. I meant what were you doing before you called," she explained.

"Well, in that case I was laying down."

"What are you doing today?" she asked.

"I'll be going to the doctor."

"What for?"

"Just want to get checked, been having some cramps but I doubt it's anything serious."

"Well, you need to be careful and don't trivialize anything about your health."

"I'm not," I answered."

"I'm just telling you because these doctors only go by what their patients tell them. And so, it is your responsibility to know what's going on with your own body."

"Thanks for the advice," I said.

"Anyhow, what's up apart from that?" Celine asked.

"Nothing new, S.O.N," I replied.

S.O.N was our way of saying same-old-nonesense.

"Are we still hanging out later?" Celine asked.

"Sure, call up Kaida and see if she wants to hang with us."

"I'm most certain that she will if she gets someone to watch the kids. When you two hook up y'all become a pair of nuts."

"Oh, don't even go there. At least we don't get drunk to the point where we talk shit and get ourselves busted."

I laughed as I remembered the incident that took place several months back.

"Ah, it was only once..."

"Hold on a sec Sher, I have a call coming in."

Silence rung in my ear while I waited for celine to come back. Then I heard a click, and Celine's voice sang through once more.

"Let me call you back later Sher, mom's on the next line."

"Alright, tell her I said 'hi'."

"Will do. Later.'

I rested the phone in its nesting place, yet my thoughts still brought me to that day. We had been at Celine's house playing cards and drinking. I had gotten drunk that night as easily as I usually did on any other occasion. I began to babble until eventually Kaida was injected with the fact that her man was a dog. He had been coming on to me for as long as they had been together. It was a good thing that Kaida had not been too much into him, and so our plan was set that very night.

The very next day he took her shopping. If I recall correctly, his name was Prince. Three days later as agreed Prince and I met at 'Side Step,' a local motel. I immediately got to the intended and blindfolded him as we got through the door. Afterwards I tied his arms to either sides of the full sized bed. When Prince's arms were secure I allowed Kaida and Celine to come in and play their parts as they assisted me in tying his legs. By the time Prince became aware of the real deal, his struggle could not allow him to get free.

We stuffed a few pillows underneath his stomach to hike his behind in the air, then cut his briefs off. He was vulnerable and open for anything. After Kaida gave Prince a lecture on being a 'good boy' we all left him there. He made ten o'clock news the next night and so it turned out that we brought him fame for a minute. I laughed to myself remembering the silly times that Celine and I shared. Still, lately she had begun to get on my nerves so I was really unsure of what would become of us.

Celine

Saturday finally came, the day that I lived for. I got out of bed, yawned, stretched and went over to the mirror to look at myself. My figure elegantly shined through my red, laced see-through lingerie that reached just below my ass. I was the proud owner of many of these because I enjoyed going to my bed feeling very sexy. My hair was combed to the back and covered with a red silk head-tie. My big brown eyes looked less tired than they were a couple days before and my skin glowed nicely from my nightly moisturizing routine.

I undressed and visually examined my body. *"Looks good,"* I decided to myself then untied my hair, and went in the shower. When I got out I made a healthy breakfast of fried eggs and chicken sausages with potato ashes and a cup of hot chocolate to last me through the beginning of my well-scheduled day. By the time I got finished with cleaning the kitchen area the clock read eleven a.m. I went to get ready to head to the mall for a few things that I needed.

The weather was a bit of a drag, but I had my car so it did not really bother me much. I grabbed the keys to my brand new gray Lexus and went through the door. My master's degree from New York University was finally paying off, and I deserved it after all those hard and tiring years in school. I sat, buckled up, and slid in one of my favorite CD, Celine Dion's "A New Day". I sang along as I turned on to Kings Highway to get to the Plaza. The rain outside had turned from heavy pours to a slight drizzle so things appeared good for my day ahead.

After I got to King's Plaza, it was not easy to find a parking since all the spots were filled. Luckily, after I circled the area twice I saw a car pulling out. Quickly, I drove over and waited as he exited and then rolled right in. As I stepped out and began walking I heard a familiar voice.

"Hi sexy, mmh-mmh-mmh! Damn, you look good!"

Although we had not seen each other in a while I knew that voice all too well.

"Hi Rob."

I turned and there he was closing the distance between us. We hugged each other.

"So what have you been up to girlie?"

Rob stared me up and down.

"I see life's been treating you good," he continued.

"I'm doing good, can't complain. How have you been? It's been a while since I last saw you," I replied.

"Went back home and spent a couple months to help straighten things out after mom passed."

"Sorry to hear about your mom."

Rob and I went to high school together our freshman year and at one point had a little crush between us. We had stayed in contact for a couple months after graduation, but then slowly stopped calling each other.

"Where are you heading?" he asked.

"Inside King's Plaza to get a few things."

"Well, give me your number so we could hang out some time."

I gave Rob my home number, we hugged, and then stepped in opposite directions.

My first stop was Bath and Body Works. The variety of aromas in there were mind boggling, but in a good way. I walked out with a medium sized shopping bag with different colors scented candles. I also bought lotions, body washes, and mists of different flavors. From The Avenue, I picked out a nice pair of black two-inch slippers that I thought would go perfectly with my gray silk dress pants and black sleeveless top for my date that night. In about an hour and a half I was finished, which was actually record time for me.

When I got home I tried my outfit. I usually liked to try an outfit before the day I plan to wear it because it might not always suit my taste after I put it on. I turned in front of the mirror to view myself from all angles before deciding that the outfit was to my taste. I loved the way my curvaceous body shined in that pants, and the slippers were a bonus finishing touch. Afterwards, I undressed and went downstairs to satisfy my thirst with a glass of water. That was when I noticed the red light flashing like a siren on my answering machine. I went over and pressed the white play button.

Beep... *"Hi baby! Just call to see how my lovely daughter is doing. Call me later."* My mom was so protective; she called so often she might as well had been living with me. I loved her so much though.

Beep... *"Hey Celine! It's Rob, just wondering if this weekend to hang out is good for you. Give me a call and let me know. My cell number is 555-444-8989. Later".*

This message surprised me a whole lot because I was not expecting him to call, especially so soon.

Beep... *"Hi my sweet, how is your day going. Was calling to hear your voice. I'll see you later."*

My heart melted when I heard Chris's voice sounding like he missed me so much. That man was rocking my world and I really liked the feeling. We had such a good connection that I felt like he was my soul mate. I snapped back to present before going deep in thoughts and went to call my mom and dad.

"Hey baby."

"Hi mom. How's everything?"

"Good and how about you?"

"I'm fine. Where's dad?"

"He went to the office earlier. Should be back any minute now. What are you up to."

"I just got back from the plaza."

"You didn't buy more lingerie, did you?"

I smiled at my known obsession.

"No mom. This time it was lotions, sprays, and candles."

"Uhm, you have a date or something?" she questioned.

I paused because somehow my mother always knew what went on in my life before I even told her. Yet, somehow I was surprised that she asked. I wanted to see what Chris and I were all about before I mentioned anything to my parents. I thought up something quick and answered her.

"Well, kinda but not really."

"What do you mean by not really honey?" she asked.

"It's nothing serious."

"I'm sure it isn't honey," she replied in a knowing tone.

"Ah come on mom, please lay off."

"I'm not on. So how long have you been going out with this person?"

"Not long. Don't remember exactly."

"Ok, so now you have amnesia?" she asked.

My mom's laughter echoed on the next end and I shook my head at her silliness. She knew that I would have called and told her the full details eventually, I usually did.

"Mom, I gotta go. Give dad a kiss for me. Love you."

"Love you too sweetie. And have fun on your not so serious date with Mr. Question mark."

"Thanks mom, I will."

I drifted off after hanging up the phone.

By the time I got up the hands on the clock emphasized that the time had shot to seven p.m. I was instantly frantic because I disliked being late for any reason at all. I cooled off my body while pinning up my hair in a sexy bun at the back of my head with a front center part. I allowed a few strands of hair to hang pass my shoulders. At seven thirty-five I was just getting in the shower. I was glad that my clothes were ready for me to just put them on. Also, I wore little make-up, which saved time in that department.

However, I still did not finish on time because when Chris rang my doorbell I was just putting some creme on my skin. I did not want to keep him waiting outside so I grabbed my robe from the bathroom door and went downstairs.

"Hi Chris, sorry I'm not ready. I just need a few more minutes to finish getting dressed. You can make yourself comfortable in the living room."

"That's fine. Take your time."

"I'll be right back."

As I walked back upstairs I could feel Chris' eyes glued to my every move. The feeling thrilled me knowing that I could demand his attention in such a way. I got to my bedroom and quickly got dressed. A few minutes later we were headed through the door.

Chris

I was thrilled with the way Celine handled herself. She was sexy and she knew it but she controlled herself and respected her body. And the way she unknowingly teased me made me yearn for her even more, yet not quite wanting to go there until she was ready. This was a difficult emotion for even me to understand, but I knew I definitely wanted to get to know her better. I got up from the car to walk Celine to her door. We kissed just as passionately as our first date and then I left with my heart dancing inside my chest.

As soon as I got home I headed straight for the bathroom, got undressed and took a dreadfully cold shower. I awoke the next day about twelve in the afternoon and decided to call up my pal Pete to see if he wanted to hit the gym early that day with me. As my thought completed my cell phone rang.

"You gonna live long man, I was just about to call you. What's up?"

"I'm thinking of hitting the gym early today, you up for it?"

"Can you read my mind or something? That's exactly what I was about to call you for."

"Great minds think alike, they always say."

Pete let out a little chuckle at the other end.

"True that. So what time did you have in mind?"

"How about we meet there in the next half-an-hour?"

"Make that an hour cuz, I kinda just got up."

"Aight, see you then."

I went downstairs and made myself a tuna sandwich and washed it down with a glass of orange juice. When I finished, I got dressed and went to pack my gym bag. Minutes later, with my sixteen ounce bottle of water in hand, I stepped out the door.

I pulled up into the lot and parked my car, retrieved my bag from the back seat and walked towards the entrance.

While scanning my membership card I noticed Monique walking up to me.

"Hi there Mr. De Angelo. Looking sexy as usual."

I smiled.

"What's up Mo'?"

We met a couple of months ago right there at the gym where she worked as an assistant trainer. She and I dated briefly, but then Monique became just one of my pals. We enjoyed the little time that we spent in each other's company.

"Nothing much. You're an early bird today huh, or did you just come by to see me?"

I laughed and she did also, "Did you see Pete come by here?"

"Nah, not yet but I guess I should be seeing him soon since you two almost never workout without each other."

I laughed again knowing that she was only speaking the truth. Pete and I were mostly always together for our routine workouts.

A couple of seconds after I got into the locker room to put away my bag, Pete walked in looking so alive and energetic. He stood five feet eleven inches, two inches taller than me. He sported single braids in a ponytail.

"What's up my man?" he asked.

"What's up with you, did you finally get a date?"

He walked up to give me a pound and a hug, which I gladly reciprocated.

"Why you trying to play me son?"

"I'm not; only asking about what's obvious."

Pete grinned from ear to ear.

"Right. Am I shining that much?"

"You don't even want to see that 'hey I got some last night after hopeless years' look on your face," I replied.

"Get outta here, can't be that bad."

"Like I said bro you don't want to see that look on your face."

He placed his black Nike bag in a locker two doors down from mine and we headed towards the floor to warm up with some push-ups before lifting any weights.

An hour had passed by the time we were done so Pete and I decided to go get a bite.

"There's a pizza shop right around the corner from here that we could walk to," Pete suggested.

"Ok, let me just put my bag in the car," I replied.

"You remember Sharon who I was trying to go out with for a while now?"

"Yeah I think so. Is she that skinny, light skinned Spanish chick?"

"Yeah, that's the one. Well, we finally went out last night and we are supposed to be going out again this weekend. But she had plans before with her girlfriend and she doesn't want to cancel. So I want you to come along on a double date with us. Her friend sounds like the perfect girl for you."

"Couldn't be man because I am already dating the perfect girl for me."

Pete stood like a statue and stared me down with furrowed brows, then began to smirk.

"Man this Celine woman is getting under your skin isn't she?"

The smirk got even more noticeable.

"Can't deny it man, she's truly something special. I think she might be the one."

Pete's look of surprise turned to complete shock.

"Come on man you telling me that it's really that serious? You sure it's not just about the pum-pum?"

The look on my face clearly sent him the message.

"Oh man, you in this deep. Don't know what to say bro."

Pete paused for a little while and then looked at me.

"If you really want this to be then I really hope she's the one for you too. You my bro and I always got your back."

He was the best pal a guy could ask for. Pete was half-American, half-Jamaican with a mouth full of foul languages. But, aside from that he was there for me, even a bit sensitive at times. No doubt he was my dawg, had been since that September day we met in high school.

Sheria

I was on my way to see Bobbi, someone I met a few weeks before. We had made plans to watch a blockbuster movie at her apartment. When I got there she had just gotten back from renting the movies. I placed my pocket book on the center table in front of me as I sat on her couch to make myself more comfortable. Bobbi went into the kitchen and brought back a bottle and two glasses.

"Did you eat yet?" she asked.

"Yeah, I had a quick bite before I left the house just now."

She poured some of the bottle's content into each glass and handed one to me. After the DVD began to load we both laid back in the chair in the livingroom and got comfortable. Bobbi and I sipped on our Hipnotiq and laughed hysterically with wonderment at the movie 'Catch Me If You Can' starring Tom Hanks and Leonardo Di Caprio. No matter how many times I saw that movie it always made me laugh just as hard as the first time.

By the end of the movie I was tipsy and suppose that she was feeling light headed also. I lifted my hand to place at the back of the chair in order to push myself upwards. However, it accidentally brushed against her right nipple. It was perky and as hard as a brick. Bobbi's body shivered and her face got flushed.

Instantly, I felt a gush of wetness between my legs. At that time we made eye contact with each other.

She raised her arm and gently ran her fingers through my curly hair. The firmness of her fingertips against my scalp sent a rush through my entire body. I gently pulled her face in and kissed. She returned my kiss while reaching to pinch my nipple. Then Bobbi got up and we both stumbled to her bedroom. The drawer of the irregular bedside table to the right of her bed held the vibrator that she used to drive me wild after she first sent me crazy with oral stimulation.

I awoke the next morning in Bobbi's arms. This time I took the instrument from the night stand and returned the favor. Being that she was already so wet it went in deep without hesitation. She moaned in excitement and that encourage me to please her even more so I fastened my pace while I explored the rest of her with my free hand. Within minutes she exploded then drove me over yonder once more with her speedy licking.

I got home and went directly to give in to sleep.

"Sex is one hell of a great feeling, but the exhaustion afterward is something wicked," I thought to myself. Then I plopped down on my bed still fully clothed. When I got up about three in the afternoon I decided to take a walk.

Chris

Things were going so well between Celine and I. Tonight was the big night for us. I knew that it would be something special because she was not just any woman, she was special to me. I had also developed a lot of respect for her because she did not just jump in the sack with me after a date or two. But she ensured that we spent time getting to know each other on a more personal level first.

Earlier I had gone to have my hair braided. I put my shower cap on my head and then went to put in one of my favorite CDs. I went back in the bathroom turned on the shower and stepped in. My song came on blasting and I sang along as I showered, "...If you want me to stay-ay, I'll never leave. If you want me to stay-ay, we'll always be. If you want me to stay..."

I gave myself enough time to get ready because I wanted this day to be special from beginning to end.

About half of an hour later I got out of the shower, dried my skin with my white towel, wrapped it around my waist, and went into my adjoining master bedroom. I had recently bought this one family three-bedroom house. When I first saw the beauty of the house I had an instant love rush. I just knew that I had to have it even though I knew that the space would not have been big enough for the size family that I wanted. I got it deciding to myself that whenever that family came along a new house would go with it. I looked around with no success to find the remote to lower the volume of the cd since I was now out of the shower. I found it laying on the rug.

My brown colored Sean John pants and matching T-shirt laid on the bed fresh from the dry cleaners. I decided to wear them with a pair of dark brown timberland boots. I put on my baby-blue pair of silk boxer shorts, got dressed, finished up with some Insurrection Reyane Tradition and headed towards my car.

Celine

Chris arrived at my door and rang the bell promptly at seven. We had decided together that seven in the evening was good timing.

"Hi honey," I said as he handed me a dozen yellow roses with a card.

"Hi there to you my sweet."

As I smelled the roses I smiled and started to indulge naughty thoughts in my head.

"What's that smell?" he asked.

I took his hand in mine and led him.

"Come and see."

He stepped in and the look on his face was one to capture as he took in the view and scents. There were rose petals leading up to the bedroom, which we would trail later on into the night. Strawberry scents filled the air from twenty candles I lit around the house about two hours before Chris was due to arrive. Also, I changed the lightbulb in the dining area to a dark, soothing blue color to set the mood. And on my set played one of my all time favorite songs, "Can I get a kiss goodnight." The Aquarius sign speaks truth about us being romantic because indeed I am more than romantic.

"This way Mr. De-Angelo," I said as I swayed my right hand in the direction of the dining area. He walked pass me I almost jumped his bones so early into the night. *"You smell so damn good and look so damn fione!"* I exclaimed.

"What was that?"

"Nothing."

Chris turned back around and I continued to watch his sexy backside. While I was all caught up with Chris this was my little secret and I wanted to trod on very carefully.

"Wow! Celine, this is very nice. I guess I am experiencing a more creative side of you."

"Yep, and hopefully more to come."

"Most definitely my sweet."

Chris could be such a charmer sometimes, but I did not want a charmer. That would not be good enough for me. I could still remember my so-called relationship with Ralph. He was such a charmer and somehow no matter how he did me wrong I would always forgive him and let him back into my heart. Finally, I had no other choice but to be strong when he left me stranded and ran off with some other woman with five hundred dollars that he convinced me to loan to him. But I was very proud of myself when he came crawling back six months later and not only did I tell him to go to hell, but I also told him that if he did not give me my money back I would hire someone to hunt him down and beat the shit out of him. He was such a sucker to fall for such stupidity, but it worked to my advantage so too bad on his part. This time around I wanted the whole package, respect, charm, love, loyalty and all those other things that matter.

Chris pulled out my chair for me and after I sat he went and took his seat that stood adjacent to mine.

"So, what did you prepare?" Chris asked.

"Well, I cooked a variety of dishes."

I pointed as I told him what each was.

"That over there in the white container is baked fish stuffed with okra, and in the green bowl right beside it is potato salad."

"Oh, you made a pineapple upside down cake. How did you know that it was my favorite?" Chris spat with glee like an excited little kid.

"I love it too, my mom used to make it for me all the time."

"Really? My mom used to make it all the time too before she passed."

Chris put a little bit of everything on his plate and really chewed down. I felt like we were old friends by the comfort that we shared being around each other.

We ate and then went into the living room to play a few games of Sorry.

"Oh!" I teased.

I sent Chris back to his starting point and took his place when he was one move from going home. I beat him in most of the rounds and was now ready to have him for desert. I took the half-empty bottle of champaign that we were drinking from and Chris and I walked hand in hand, barefooted on the rose petals along the pathway up the stairs. My bedroom was also covered with rose petals; white ones on the floor and pink mixed with white covered the bed. I knew that it was not Christmastime, still I placed a mistletoe in the bedroom door entrance. He noticed it and played along.

"Celine you are a beautiful woman and the kiss that comes next is not only because of the mistletoe above our heads. But also because I hope this is part of a blooming phase of something special between us."

"Oh Chri..."

Before I could finish my sentence he lifted me off the floor with a gigantic swoop and delivered a tantalizing whip of tongue action. He carried me over to the bed and gently placed me down. By that time I was high from natural hormone overdose. I kneeled on the bed and lifted his shirt over his muscular shoulders. We had hugged many times before, however, it was nothing close to the intensity of fire between our bare skins at that moment. He rubbed my breasts with his palms and played with my nipples between his thumbs and forefingers. I was in ecstasy and seriously wanted him to enter me that very moment. But I guess his intention was to have me beg. Chris pushed me back onto the bed and starting kissing my face and neck. Then he started south conquering my breasts then trailing along the center of my stomach. The nibbling feeling that overtook my navel was so sensuous and drove me even wilder as he continued his mind-boggling journey down.

"Ahh!" I started to moan.

He kissed the hairless top of my vagina and then went to trail along the insides of my thighs and continued going. Then when he got to my toes, he licked each painted one.

"Oh Chris...," I begged through labored breathing. I was unable to wait any longer so I opened my legs wider, and impatiently anticipated feeling him inside me.

Sheria

My heart was just as heavy as the stack of paperwork that laid on my desk. I could not find the strength to do any of the work that I got paid to do. I knew well enough that if I did not 'move it' soon, miss-large-and-in-charge would surely step on my heels. Yet, no matter how much I tried to push myself the motivation I needed just was not there. I got up from my desk and paced the floor of my semi-private cubicle. My mind still would not put me at ease.

Lately, I had been having thoughts about where I was leading myself in life. For the most part I enjoyed my life and did not think that I needed anything more. But, sometimes some dreadful thoughts pushed regretful scenes in my mind's forefront. At those times I found myself ashamed of the things that I did. Yet, during the acts I have no remorse or sorrow at all.

"Sheria?"

I was brought back to reality by the deep voice of Bea a.k.a miss-large-and-in-charge. I spun around and met her large eyes rummaging through my desk.

"Can I help you with something?" I asked her as kindly as my spirit would allow.

"Yes, I need that letter with the estimate for Mr. Brian."

"I sent it to him yesterday," I confirmed.

"Well, he said that he did not get it. This time I will feel more comfortable doing it myself being that someone is slacking up around here. So can I please have the original so that I may fax it to him?"

"Sure, I'll bring it to you in a few," I said.

God was on her side was all I could say for me not pouncing on her right after her smart remark.

"Make it quick I have other things to do," she continued.

Bea, tall, slender, Spanish chick with a low haircut. Perhaps her mother came short on the spelling of bitch as her name. She rolled her ass away down the hall.

"Make it quick..." I mocked.

I began to look for the paper as soon as she was out of sight. My efforts later proved to be futile. I sat by my desk and drifted demanding my mind to remind me of where I had put the paper. Then like a falling mountain it hit me that I had not even drafted the letter to begin with. I had intended to when something else came up and got caught in the way. I got up frantically and tried to save my ass.

My mind had been straying lately. I knew I had to get back on track before I was shipped out. The only problem was that I had not figured out what was wrong with me yet. And no one could fix something without knowing what was wrong in the first place. Loneliness engulfed me as I fought against something inside of me, fought strong for my survival.

Celine

"Hello"

I balanced the phone between my ear and shoulder.
"Hey Celine, what's up?"

It was Rob. He had been calling quite a lot lately and it might have looked as though I was ignoring him, but I was not. With my time split mostly between my work, myself, Chris and Sheria there was no time left to hang out with him like he wanted.

"Nothing much, what's going on?" I asked.

"Calling to see if you want to catch a movie or have a drink or something."

He asked that question as if I had not turned him down so many times before. However, I had begun to feel guilty so I decided to try to squeeze in a little time to spend with him. After all we used to hang out a lot in school.

"Not a movie, how about lunch some time?" I suggested.

"Great, is tomorrow good?"

Although I thought he would have waited like at least until next week or so, I told him that it was fine.

"So I'll call you in the morning to let you know what time to meet me and where," I said.

"Ok bye."

I pressed the end button, and then pressed talk again.

"Hi my sweet."

Chris picked up on the first ring.

"Hi baby!"

"I was just about to call you."

"Guess we both have incredible minds."

I smiled to myself because I liked the way things had been going smoothly between us since the beginning.

"I guess so baby. So, what's up?"

"Calling to see what you have planned for your night."

"Well, I was hoping that we could chill, watch a movie and eat home made popcorn."

"That sound nice. I could be there in like the next hour, is that good?"

"Yeah, I'll be waiting."

"Ok I'll see you soon."

As soon as we were done talking on the phone I went to prepare myself. I was already falling for Chris and my main concern was that he would not break my heart.

I browsed through my closet wondering what to wear. Finally, after about ten minutes I narrowed it down to a red and white polka dot sleeveless dress or a black sheer top with a ankle length skirt with two splits on the sides. Either one would have been good for the Summer night. I went into the shower with the intention that by the time I was done I would be able to decide which of the two outfits to wear. Usually, I would wear my hair down, but that night I pinned it back in a roll. I slipped on the polka dot dress and put on some white shoes, grabbed my keys and left the house.

The traffic was very much congested and that dampened my spirits. But I was cheered that it was Thursday, which meant that I was only one day away from the weekend. I was driving at about ten or less miles per hour at different periods. I was competing with Celine Dion's voice blasting through my speakers, when I glimpsed some kind of confusion ahead. About eight cars ahead of me I saw the blur of some kind of raucous going on. I got closer and the picture became more clear to me.

A naked man was running along the side of the road with one hand covering his private area and the other covering his ass. He looked very scared as a woman looking to be a little over three hundred pounds, twice his size, ran behind him trying hopelessly to catch him. Then right before I passed them I saw a skinny light skinned female jump on the big woman's back dragging off her wig to reveal a bald with small patches of strands laid around the edges. I knew that must have been a regretful move for that woman. I watched as the three hundred-pound woman swung her around, threw her about two feet away, ran and jumped on her. Although it was a serious situation, I had to laugh to myself at how crazy the whole scene looked.

It took me a next fifteen minutes to get to Chris's house after I witnessed that incident. I opened his white metal gate and walked a little distance along a paved pathway to get to his door. I rang the bell and waited less than a minute before his smiling face appeared.

"Hi honey, what took you so long?"

I looked at my watch and realized that it was already nine o'clock, almost one hour from the time I said I would have been there.

"Traffic was unusually heavy."

He pulled me forward and kissed me softly on the forehead.

"Are you ready to eat?"

"Boy am I! What did you cook?"

"Come and see for yourself."

He took my hand in his and led me to the dining room. The table was decorated with a variety of foods including rice and beans, fried sweet plantains, jerked chicken, and a vegetable salad.

"Where did you learn to throw down so good?"

"My mom taught me to cook; I guess that's the advantage of being the only child and a son. She was a cooking fanatic. She enjoyed watching the cooking channels and preparing a variety of foods. This meal I prepared is mostly a Jamaican dish."

Chris and I sat and I really enjoyed the food.

"You've got some skillz boy 'cause this grub sure tastes good."

"Thanks."

Ringgg! Ringgg!

"Excuse me for a minute Celine."

"Sure go ahead."

"Hello?"

"Hey man."

"What's up cuz?"

"I'm here bored as a mother. Calling to see if you wanna play some ball or something dude."

"Can't, Celine's here right now."

"Maan. Looks like I'm gon have to find me a honey too."

We both chuckled.

"Aight son I'll give you a call tomorrow," he said.

Within the next two minutes we were in the living room. Chris turned on the radio to 106.7 lite fm and immediately Shania Twain's voice floated in.

"Do you want some ice cream, I have some chocolate flavor in the refrigerator."

"You have got to be kidding me. After all that food I'm way too stuffed for anything else."

"Well, just a thought."

We snuggled on the couch and chatted for the remainder of the night. Chris and I were getting very close, still fear ruled my heart. I wondered how far we would get.

Celine

Rob and I met at 'Azafran,' a local hot spot for Spanish foods. It was not too far away from my job out on Worth Street. When I arrived and noticed that he had not showed up yet, I got a table for us and browsed through my menu. About two minutes later he walked in.

"Hey Celine!"

He walked up and greeted me with a kiss on the cheek. It made me feel uncomfortable, but I just brushed it off instead of saying anything. Besides, he was half Hispanic and I knew that cheek kisses were traditional greetings for them.

"Hey Rob, what's up?"

He took a seat in the chair across from me and picked up the menu that sat in front of him on the table.

"So, what have you tried here before that you would recommend for me?" he asked.

"I have not eaten here before. But I've heard good things about them."

"Ok, let me see what they have to offer."

By the time the waiter came to take our orders I was absolutely ready.

"I'll have the roasted fat-free duck breast marinated in honey and Dijon sauce," I stated as my glands began salivating.

"I'll take the same," Rob said.

"So how have you been Celine?" Rob asked after the waiter left.

"I've been doing good."

"Where do you work?"

"I work at a law office just a few block down into Manhattan and soon plan to branch off on my own."

"So I can come to you for all my legal advice huh?"

"Sure," I smiled, "So how about you?"

"I manage a bar out in Flushing, Queens. It's been pretty good. But somewhere in the future I hope to move on to my own business."

"That's nice," I replied.

"Yeah, I'm in the process right now of getting my resources together."

I studied his curly black hair as he ran his fingers through while speaking to me. It crossed my mind how habitual that was for him ever since back in high school. I checked out his features. He was dark skinned, and about one hundred and thirty-five pounds at five feet five inches tall. Not so handsome, yet not ugly either as his charm and muscle built made up for what he lacked in facial appearance.

Just then the tall, lanky, dark-skinned waiter returned with our meals.

"Do enjoy," he said.

"Thank you," we both said in unison.

For the next fifteen minutes as we ate we chattered on different topics and then parted. My lunch date with Rob did not seem such a drag as I had expected. Instead, I enjoyed his company. Rob had a wild sense of humor and I could not remember the last time that I had laughed so uncontrollably. He left me in wonder about whether we met again by chance or intent.

Chris

Things always got hectic for me this time of the year. Once again the time had come for me to look over my budget in details. Over the past couple years, sales had gone up and either stayed the same or inflated. The turning point for this success happened after two full years of loss where I had even been tempted to give up. But luckily, I had good friends who pushed me, so I stayed put, and soon enough it all happened for me. Also, I knew I had to make mom proud even though she was in heaven. I was at the point now where I was ready to even invest into something else, but I was not sure I wanted to branch out with another store yet.

My laptop sat in the center of my desk and I sat in front of it trying to finalize the total of my expenses.

Ring! Ring! Ring! Ri...

"Hey, what up man?" I answered.

"Wat up wid yu bwoy?" Pete asked.

I smiled, shook my head and thought, *"there he goes with that Jamaican slang again."*

"Man I'm just here fixing my finances. Seems like yesterday I did the last adjustments."

Pete started to laugh.

"This time is usually hectic, isn't it?"

"Hachoo."

"Bless you man. That allergy crap acting up again?"

"Yeah, I've been taking this over the counter drug, but that shit hardly work."

"I think Alley's doctor gave her something called Zyrtec D, maybe you should try it."

"We'll see, you know how I hate going to those damn doctors."

"Anyway, I called to tell you there's a little jam happening next Friday, and Jay wants us to just hang out there instead of throwing him a bachelor party."

"What's up, wifey trippin'?"

"Yeah son, she ain't even trying to hear it. So you down?"

"Sure man, no doubt."

"Aight then catch you later."

I looked at the clock that stood on the wall to my left and saw that it was one p.m. Celine had left yesterday and I was already missing her like crazy. I could hardly function and did not know how I was going to make it through the rest of the three days she would be away. It seemed so much more than four months since we had been seeing each other. Momentarily, the vibration of my phone made me aware of an incoming call. I looked at the caller id and saw an unusual area-code and number.

"Hi honey!" I answered, ecstatic to hear from her.

"How did you know it was me?" she laughed.

"Who else would it be? I'm glad you called, was just thinking about you."

"Oh yeah? What were you thinking?" Celine asked.

"That I miss you."

"Oh, do you now?" she asked.

She spoke in that sexy voice that always drove me crazy.

"Of course baby, I love you."

"Well, the feeling is most definitely mutual."

We spent one hour on the phone talking about nothing in particular. I was far from finishing up, but after talking to Celine I decided to go to the gym to work off some of my built up tension I had from missing her so. I continuously wondered why I was so attracted to Celine. The attention that she drew form me was unlike anything that I knew. My mind kept busy as I tried hard to figure out what would become of us.

Celine

I awoke at about eight am to the smell of eggs and bacon. The nice Florida sun was already pelting through the thin red curtains of the guestroom I always stayed in whenever I visited. I involuntarily blinked a few times to adjust my eyes to the light of the room. Then I got off the bed, yawned, and stretched. I went to the bathroom down the hall to do the first emptying of my bladder for the day and brush my teeth. Within five minutes, still wearing my silk shorts pajamas, I headed down the stairs allowing the aroma of food to lead me.

"Well, well, well look who finally decided to join us today."

"Daddy it is only eight twenty. You and ma be getting up way too early for me. Besides, I *am* on vacation."

"So I guess your mother's cooking dragged you down here huh?"

"You know it! Momma's cooking could drag anyone from sleep no matter how tired they are."

My father sat on the couch in the living room. But I realized that he had already showered and was dressed to go out.

"Are you going out daddy?"

"Yes, I have to run down to the office to do something. I should be back in a few hours."

"So early?"

"The earlier the better for me," he replied.

"Well, I think mom and I are going to the mall. Maybe later the three of us could dine out or go catch a movie."

"Sure, that's fine with me."

My parents had moved to Kissimmee three years previous. By then they were more than settled and enjoyed the beauty of being free and able to afford a good lifestyle. I went into the kitchen to see my mother balancing two plates in her hands and transporting them to the dining area.

"Good morning ma, how are you?"

"Morning sweetie did you sleep good?"

"Yes, I did. Could have slept a little while longer though, but the tantalizing scents of your cooking stimulated my glands."

She grinned. I followed her into the dining room and watched as she placed the plates down.

"You are just something else Celine, and I love you."

"I love you too mom."

I went over and hugged her.

"Breakfast is ready. You go sit while I get your father."

We all sat and munched on fried eggs, bacon strips, and french toasts, with a fruit salad consisting of mangoes, strawberries, and apples. To drink we each had a glass of Sunny Delight orange juice.

"Mom, are we still going to the mall today?" I asked while taking a whole strawberry in my mouth.

"Sure honey, wherever you want to go."

"Ok and I also told dad that maybe the three of us could catch a movie later."

"Sure. That works for me," she agreed.

We finished eating, then dad left for his office and mom went to get ready. I decided to call Chris. As I sat in the living room I looked around loving my mother's decorating talent. Smooth, spongy soft, thick, white carpet covered the floors. The three-piece couch set that sat beautifully in the center of the room was creme with pine wood base. The wall unit was also made from pine wood and stood opposite a fireplace. Above the fireplace sat one of the most cherished and memorable pictures of our family. It was a gigantic sized wedding picture of mom and dad. Gracing each side was one picture of me as a baby and another of me as an adult. There were two paintings facing each other from opposite walls. My mother was a fanatic when it came to paintings. She had a separate little room decorated with all her "prize" collections, as she called them.

I picked up the phone from the wooded table beside the couch and my fingers took on a excited life of their own as they dialed Chris's number. I hung up with disappointment, but decided to try back in a few minutes. Just as I attempted to get up the phone rang.

"Hello?" I answered.

"Hi my sweet."

He sounded breathless, yet happy.

"Hey beau, just tried to call you."

"I know. Went outside to pick up the mail and caught the last ring on my way in."

"So what's up? How are things there?" I asked.

"Ok, just not as good as it would have been if you were here. I really miss you," he replied.

"I miss you too honey, but it's just one more day."

"One day's just as much a killer, but I'll try to make it. So how are your parents doing?" Chris asked.

"They're ok, mom and I are going shopping in a little while."

There was a short pause as I listened to see if mom had gotten out the shower.

"Let me call you back later Chris. I think mom's almost ready."

"Got to go so soon?" he asked with a disappointed tone.

"Yeah, but I promise I'll call you later."

"Ok, I love you. And have fun," he said.

"Love you too."

Chris

I picked up Celine promptly at seven fifteen just in case we had any delays so that we could still make our eight o'clock reservation. She wore a nice red evening dress that flowed to her ankles. With that she wore matching heels that accentuated her painted toes. The tiny red purse she carried just showed the Cinderella in her even more.

"Hi my sweet. You look beautiful," I complimented.

"Well, thank you. And I must say the same of you handsome."

I took her hand and kissed the back of it.

"What's that for?" Celine asked.

"That my dear is for the pleasure of being with you tonight."

"Oh Chris, you need to stop."

She blushed and her lips widened in an incredible Julia Roberts smile.

"Not until you promise me one thing," I said.

"What's that?" she asked with raised brows.

"That you'll always be in my life."

"I really want that too so much."

"So go ahead and promise me."

Tears welled in Celine's brown eyes as she stared at me lovingly, yet unsure of what all that meant.

"I promise. Chris, I love you."

I did not respond but I took her hand and interlocked her fingers with mine.

Traffic was good and we got to the restaurant at seven fifty. The special secluded area that I chose had silk curtains ensuring our privacy. Instead of having someone play for us I asked to have a plug available to keep the moment between just us two. I had dropped the radio off along with the CD, and asked to have it set up prior to our arrival.

As soon as she sat I pressed play.

"*Endless Love*" by Diana Ross and Lionel Richie floated in the air.

"This song is a dedication to you my sweet," I said.

"Thank you, it's one of my all time favorites."

Celine wore a questioning look on her face. I went over to her side of the table and knelt down beside her.

"I thought that I could wait, but I don't want to inhale another breath of air until I know you'll be mine," I said.

Confusion and excitement filled her face at once.

"I love you Celine and," Mark Anthony's song came on but only repeated the most important part I wanted, "will you marry, marry me...?"

She covered her face and started to cry silent tears.

"This is supposed to be a happy moment my sweet. Please don't cry."

"I know. I am happy, sooo happy," she cried.

"So are you going to answer the question?" I asked.

Her eyes glossed and danced with a smile on her beautiful face as she answered, "yes."

"Yes you're going to answer me or yes you'll marry me?" I asked again.

She laughed.

"Yes, I will marry you silly."

Celine flung her arms around my neck and seduced my tongue and lips.

"I love you Celine."

"Love you too Chris."

We enjoyed a wonderful meal, more melodious music, and created some unforgettable memories before and after we left 'our spot'.

Celine

Chris and I had a wonderful time the night before. When I woke up the next morning at his house, he had breakfast waiting for me. There was boiled eggs, ham, toasts, and syrup with coffee on the tray. A heart made from red paper accompanied my breakfast; it read, "I'm glad you said yes". My heart blushed instantly and a feeling came over me that that was it. The love that I had been waiting for.

But, it was time to put last night to the side of my mind as I prepared myself to meet Rob. We had decided to meet at a coffeehouse close to Fourteenth Street. When I walked in I saw Rob walking to find a seat also, so I assumed I got there right on time. He finally sat, then noticed me walking towards him and got right back up.

"Hi Celine, how are you?"

His eyes glistened with excitement as he took my hand and kissed it.

"Hey, I'm fine. How 'bout you?"

"I'm good now that I finally got a chance to spend some time with you."

"Stop," I said playfully yet meaning it.

Rob looked handsome in his light blue polo shirt and blue knee length jean shorts with black sandals.

"I'm dead ass girl, you know that."

We sat and made a lite order; a plain vegetable salad for me and he had a sandwich. I drank iced-tea, while Rob had a large cappuccino.

"So how was your trip?" he questioned.

"It was really nice to see my parents."

"That's nice. I miss my moms sometimes, but she's in a better place so I have to be glad.

After we finished our meal we went for a walk in a nearby park. Rob was a very nice person to converse with, and he had a special charm about him that any woman would find irresistible. I really don't remember how the conversation came up but we were talking about why people cheat on their spouses.

"I think that if it's in the individual, it will always be there."

I felt very strongly about that point.

"I think that the chances of recurrence is greater for a man, however, it's pretty slim regardless of whom the person is. I just believe that once a cheater, always a cheater," I continued.

"I don't think so and I do believe that I smell bias here. Why do you think the chances are greater among males?" Rob asked.

"Because they are often less sensitive, still feel the need to maintain their macho attitudes, and most times that's the only way they know how."

"Well, I think that it depends on the individual and how much you love your spouse."

"So in other words are you saying that a person won't cheat if he or she is in love with one's spouse?" I asked.

"No, that is definitely not what I'm saying. I just think that cheating somehow stems from a person's relationship at home with one's mate."

Rob and I debated back and forth for a good bit before we finally accepted that we would not agree. When it was time to go back to work we parted company and went in separate directions.

I do not know why that particular song popped in my head, yet I went back to my job singing 'Mrs. Jones'.

Chris

It was going on two weeks since I proposed to Celine and things were looking better than ever for us. I had been surprised at how easily things were falling into place between us, and how deeply I felt for her. I could not even begin to explain it. When I told Pete he was already a step ahead of me. I can still remember his exact words.

"Man tell me something I don't know!"

"What you talking 'bout son? This just happened last night, so how could you know?"

"Bro I knew it was coming, you never acted this way about a woman before. Just too good to let go I guess."

"I know that's right. I love her man."

"Son, like I said tell me something I don't know because that shit is written all over you."

We both fell out in laughter from that one. Sometimes it was still hard to believe that I found such a wonderful woman to share my life with.

Since the proposal we had been spending more time sleeping by each other's house. It had been two nights though since we had been together. Tonight would make the third being that I had plans to hang out with the guys to celebrate a bachelorhood in the demolishing stage. I seriously thought of ditching them to go be with my baby, I missed her. But in the end I could not dog my boys that way, a promise was a promise.

Seven of us gathered at 'Club NY', basically to have drinks, chat, and whatever else except get the groom involved with any females. We had strict warning about that and we all knew that Pam was not the one to mess with. The atmosphere inside was nice. There were females from different backgrounds walking in and instantly marking their territories.

"Yo check out that chica at eleven o'clock in that red mini skirt showing most of what her momma gave her."

This was Greg speaking. He was the biggest womanizer of the group and the dog of all dogs.

"Dyyam mamma," he continued.

"Son she really do have some curves on her, but I would only hit it on a temp basis," said Hardy.

"You can easily tell who're the money grabber from who's here to have a good time," I said.

"And none these are in here to just chill."

Pete's vocal confidence showed he knew what he was talking about.

"Ain't that right. These chickens just want a baby daddy or some quick money."

This was Hardy who was second in line after Greg in dogging. We slapped palms and laughed. By that time we were all on our third beers, and some of us were getting tipsy already.

At one thirty just when we were ready to break off, she showed up out of nowhere. The sight of her almost caused me to choke on my last swallow of party drink. The instant that I spot her in the entrance I could tell that she saw me too, and that her destination was where I stood. She stepped slowly towards me like a super-model who knew she was all that. A few eyes darted and stayed sharply in her direction as she continued her journey.

Her shapely hips swayed sexily from side to side with each step that she took. She wore a tight pink mini-mini dress that stopped right underneath her ass. The matching purse she carried topped off her outfit along with her pink and black strapped up slippers. I cursed myself for the excitement that I felt from seeing her again. When she stopped in front of me my eyes immediately appreciated the nice Halle Berry haircut that she rocked. She placed one leg forward with heel turned inward. Then her right hand found her hip to finish the pose.

"Well, hi there handsome, long time no see."

"Brenda?"

"Yeah Pete, it's the one and only me in the flesh."

"I thought you moved away to Atlanta."

"Yeah, I did. But am here now."

I was still totally stunned to see her again as she and Pete kept conversing. Finally, she gazed my way again, this time her attention was undivided.

"Well, aren't you happy to see me? Cat got your tongue?" she asked.

"No the cat don't have my tongue, I'm fine."

"Well, what's the matter aren't you happy to see me?"

I could hardly believe the nerve of her to ask me that question in the first place much more to actually repeat it.

"Should I be?" I demanded.

"Yeah, remember I was the one you wanted to make wifey? Your one and only beau?"

"That was then and that's all in the past."

"So it's like that now, huh?"

"Like what Brenda? You were the one who made a choice and I was the one who was stuck with it."

"That's behind us Chris, come on."

"Nice to see you again, but we were just on our way out. Yo Pete, you ready man?"

"Sure."

His voice gave off hesitancy as he stood there looking at her in disbelief.

"Can I talk with you in private Chris?" Brenda asked.

"I don't think so."

"Just a few minutes. I'm really glad I ran into you because this is important and I've been trying to reach you about it."

"It's okay man I'll just wait for you over there," Pete urged.

"You could go ahead bro., I'll just catch up with you later."

"You sure?"

Pete was my pal and he always had my back, but this was something I needed to handle on my own.

"Yeah, I'll call you tomorrow."

"Aight, be cool."

He came closer and we gave each other a pound and hugged before he told Brenda bye and left.

I stood there for the first minute debating whether to walk off on her the way she had walked out on me. But that was childish, besides I still had unanswered questions that haunted me every now and then. I figured that that was my chance to get some answers.

"So what's up? Make it quick," I snapped.

"You don't have to be rude. At least have a drink with me," she said.

Brenda poked out her bottom lip the way she always did to get through to me. I contemplated saying no, however, thought that perhaps what she had to say would call for it.

"Alright, just one and then I'm out."

Brenda ordered Remy Red while I had some scotch on the rocks. Almost two minutes passed after getting our drinks and she still had not said a word. She sat there playing with her glass seemingly in deep thoughts.

"So what you gotta talk about?" I finally asked.

Seeing her again stirred up some bitter anger inside of me because back then I just knew she was the one. I just knew we could have had something special, but Brenda was not willing to give up her hoeing ways.

"I don't really know where to start telling you this," she began.

"Just say it. There's never any easy way to tell something difficult to explain in the first place."

"I had a baby."

"And? What's that got to do with me?"

"He's five years old."

"Huh-huh?"

I know I must have had a silly look on my face because in my mind I just wanted her to get to the damn point and tell me what the heck any of her shit had to do with me.

"His name is Christan De-Angelo."

"No, no way," I shook my head and waved my arm uncontrollably, "Don't try to tell me any bullshit now that the child is mine."

Tears came to her eyes and her face became flushed. I looked at her and empathy began to swim inside my heart.

"Hey, am sorry."

"It's okay I know this is too much too soon for you to deal with. I hid the pregnancy from you. But when I wanted to contact you afterwards I was not sure of how you'd react so I never did," she explained.

I was in a totally different world by then as I felt confusion on top of tipsiness stirring my mind. The quickness with which I stood caused me to stumble into the barstool to my left. Brenda shot up off her stool and was by my side supporting me in no time.

"You ok?" she asked.

"Yeah, I'm fine."

I lied because the last thing I wanted was to be in a vulnerable position around her.

"No you're not, let me take you home."

"Ok."

I did not expect that there would have been any harm in her taking me home so I agreed. Besides, I was in no condition to drive.

About half an hour later Brenda pulled over and assisted me out of the car. I started to take out my keys when I realized she had hers ready to open the door.

"What are you doing? That's not my keys."

"I know."

When I looked up I realized through droopy eyes that I was in a place that had no familiarity to me.

"Hey, where the heck are we?" I demanded.

"I took you by my house since it's much closer and you don't feel or look too good."

I was too tired and drained to argue so I waited for her to finish opening the door so I could go in. My steps through the door were crooked and so when I got inside I immediately leaned against the wall. My eyes wandered around for a place to just flop down.

"Where's your couch?" I asked.

"Don't have one. The bedroom is to your left a little way down that hall. Wait up and I'll show you."

I had no choice but to lean against the wall of the hallway and wait. Another step and I was bound to hit my face on the floor.

"Come this way, hold on to me."

Brenda wrapped her arm around me and supported me to the bed.

"You should take a shower, you'll feel a whole lot better."

"I do feel like shit but I don't think I could make it in there."

I was as drunk as an alcoholic, but I still had some sense left in me. Although I had suspicions in my mind, I doubt that she was really up to anything. Besides, she did not want me before so why should she want me then.

"On second thoughts where's your shower? I think I'll take a quick one," I said.

"On the other side of the hallway facing the bedroom."

"Ok thanks."

I got up and staggered to the bathroom. The place looked dull and broken down to me. However, I thought it might have been my imagination since she was always a high maintenance woman who would not dare be caught dead in a place less than fitting for her character. I bolted the lock on the door before I went into the shower. Within ten minutes I walked out with a towel wrapped around my waist while Brenda walked in.

"There's some mint tea over there on the side table, drink it up. I'll be right back," she instructed.

"Ok, thanks."

By the time she came out of the shower I was done with the tea.

"How do you feel now?"

"A little better, but my head is pounding like crazy."

"Give it a while longer for the feeling to wear off."

Since that day she left I had been mad at her. And though I was still mad, damn if I didn't notice she was just as sexy as she was when we were together. She wore a little lime green colored shorts made of a stretchy material that sucked on to her every curve. The black revealing tube top was no different as it caressed her oversized boobs. She always kept long hair, but that nice, short do that she sported was fitting her oval face just right. I could not lie the girl was damn flyy with two ys. My other head started to pound as it tried to bust through my pants like some damn hulk. I had to quicken my reflexes and throw the covers over my lap so Brenda would not notice my growing excitement. Guess I was too late because in an instant there she was bare breasted in front of me trying to take advantage. Deep down I was mad at my weak ass as I thought about the sexual heat that was about to take place. But on the surface I was very thirsty and I knew she would do a good job at quenching that thirst like she had so many other times before.

"You want some of this?"

Brenda pushed her boobs up in my face almost stopping air from entering my nostrils. She was every man's dream in bed, too bad that's all she could be.

"Answer me! I said do you want some of this?" she aggressed.

The wild side of me instantly took over as I joined her in the role-play that we did well together multiple times before.

"Hell yeah!"

"I didn't hear you."

"Yeah baby."

"I thought so!"

Without hesitation she pushed her boobs deeper in my face. I began to suck on them and she moaned excitedly. After a brief tonging session she gave me head and I came. Knowing how to do the job right Brenda started to tease me again trailing my body, rubbing her huge breasts all over my face, and all that good stuff. As soon as she felt my dick hard again she turned around on the wall and cocked up her ass.

"Spanking time baby!" she announced.

Brenda spread her legs and bent over some more to give me the best access possible.

"Fuck me baby! Fuck me good!"

I did.

"Whose ass is this?" I yelled.

"It's yours baby."

"Whose?"

As I claimed her my pace became faster. I tried desperately to plunge deeper and deeper inside. She loved it like that, and I used to love giving it to her that way.

"You..r..s ba...ba...by."

Celine

For the past two and a half weeks it seemed that Chris had distanced himself from me. As the two first weeks passed I remained understanding when he kept telling me that the bookstore required a lot of his attention right then. On some evenings he would come over, spend an half of an hour and then disappear into the night with excuses of unfinished work to do. But, the past three days had been hell for me as I cried my eyes dry at night wondering what had become of us.

Three days previous was the last time that I had seen Chris and at times when I called I was unable to reach him. Yet, whenever he called back we only spoke briefly before he cut through our already shortened conversations. Fed-up could hardly explain my feelings by then.

I really was in no mood to have company, however, Rob insisted on a Blockbuster night. In the end I was glad that I agreed because his great sense of humor along with the movie did a good job of entertaining me momentarily.

"So, didn't you have fun?" Rob asked.

"Yeah, a lot. I know I did not want the company, but I am grateful that you insisted."

"I had fun too, I always do with you. You're a very special woman Celine."

"Thank you."

The truth was I really did enjoy spending time with Rob. There was something special about him that caused me to relax and be myself when he was around. Sometimes I felt guilty because I did not think Chris would approve of me having so much fun with another man. Do not get me wrong, the times I spent with Chris were very unforgettable, still I had begun to feel an unexplainable connection to Rob. He was there for me when I needed a shoulder to lean on and this was one of those occasions. I watched while Rob ran his fingers through his hair as was so common for him. Then the fade of a one inch cut above his left eyebrow crossed my vision. I wondered about the cause of it as Rob kept his gaze on me with a wide smile. I smiled back not wanting to make him become unsettled. A silent, awkward moment that made me unsure of its innocence washed over us; I had to break it.

"Ok, so I'm going to turn in now. I guess we'll talk tomorrow."

Without a reply Rob got up and prepared himself. He then led the way and I followed him to the door.

We hugged as usual whenever we greeted or parted from each other. That night, however, the hug seemed peculiarly different. It was tighter, yet warm and comforting at the same time. And instead of its usual place on my cheek, the kiss of his tender lips greeted my vulnerable forehead. A shiver filled my insides and I hoped that Rob had not seen my mixed gesture.

"Do you want me to stay with you tonight? I'll sleep on the couch," he offered.

"No, thanks."

"You sure? I really don't mind. You still don't look too good," he insisted.

"Yeah, I'll be fine," I refused once more.

"Ok take care of yourself babe. I'll call you tomorrow."
"Bye Rob, get home safe."
"Ok."

Sheria

After work Celine and I met at the Mall as planned. It had become a tradition for us to do Christmas shopping earlier ever since Celine began dragging me along with her a few years back.

"So which one do you want to hit first?" I asked already knowing her answer. I mouthed along as her words came out.

"Sexy Slithering Strings, you know that."

Every year I would ask regardless and every year she would tell me the same thing.

"Don't you get tired of buying drawers?" I asked her.

"No, never that," Celine replied with much attitude.

"Alright, well let's go."

We turned left, took the escalator one flight up and turned right. After walking passed a few other stores we saw the bold sign welcoming us.

It was Celine's tendency to find something to finger as soon as we got to the door of the store. However, this time she barely noticed anything as she walked around touching a piece here and there but not being affected by any. My concern for my best friend pushed me back to her. The isles were very scanty so I felt that we could talk there.

"What's the matter Celine?" I asked

"With what?" she replied.

"You, you don't look at ease. Something wrong?"

"Well, kinda, but it's no big deal."

"Don't even give me that. The least you could do is allow me to be there for you the way you always want to be there for me," I said.

"I'm sorry, you're right. Chris just haven't been acting right lately."

"How so?"

"He has been distant. He comes around maybe two or three days in the week and don't even spend much time."

"What do you think it is, did you guys have an argument or something?"

"No. Actually, that's what I can't understand, his proposal was right before he started acting this way."

"Oh honey, why don't you speak to him about it?" I asked.

"I'm scared that he regrets proposing to me."

"I doubt that. I could tell since the beginning that you guys had something special going on. I bet it turns out to be so simple. I really think that you should just talk to him about it."

"I might as well. I guess I'll just have to face whatever it is."

I could tell that her mind was really preoccupied with what was happening between her and Chris.

"Honey you look stressed, and for you not to go crazy over this piece is enough evidence."

I held up a pearly-pink, laced, crotch-less lingerie that I had become attracted to.

Celine smiled, "girl, stop kidding! That's your type, not mine."

That was my type of lingerie. But my purpose of putting a smile on her face was accomplished, if only for a minute.

"We'll do the shopping another day. Just please go and give Chris a call. Breaks my heart to see you so sad."

"Are you sure?" she asked.

"Of course. Let's go."

I pulled Celine's hand in mine, interlaced our fingers and we walked out the mall and into our cars.

"I'll call you later Sher."

"Alright Celine. Love you girl."

"Love you too."

As I drove on my way home my mind wandered on the reason why I liked my life the way it was. I did not have to deal with any crap because there were no commitments, and none to be made. Someone always gets hurt that way. My way was much safer to the emotions. Meet, have sex, end of the relationship, everybody's happy. I smiled to myself as I called up Nick, I had fantasies that I wanted to make come true that night.

Chris

"We need to talk Chris I can't go on this way."

It was about ten o'clock at night when Celine called me. She sounded very serious. And though I was reluctant because of lack of explanation for my *ill* behavior, her call brought relief to me. I myself knew that eventually we had to speak with each other and there was no way around it. But at the same time I was not sure how to initiate a conversation between us, especially since I had been acting stupidly towards her. Celine was a wonderful woman and hurting her was nowhere on my agenda, and so I wanted to prove that to her. But that would have meant lying to her and I was not sure that that was the best way to start a commitment with someone I loved.

All those nights that I avoided Celine, I really had been stressed because of the process of opening my new store. But most of the stress came from trying to ignore and get passed that one night. I can still remember the headache it caused me as I rushed, confused and hopeful two days later to get an HIV test. Brenda looked fine and all, but those HIV medicines were more improved, slowing down the sickness process, although the disease was still fatal.

I remember when I went for my results. Guilt rushed through me as I sat in the waiting room with all eyes settled on me. They all seemed to have known the shameful sin that I had committed. Most of the men

smiled giving me the thumbs up sign saying, *"playa, playa, you tap that ass cuz."* But all the women looked at me with red murderous eyes that said, *"you bastard, I put so much into this relationship, into you and this is how you thank and appreciate me? By mother-fucking sleeping with another woman?"*
"Mr. De-Angelo?"
A uniformed woman had called my name and snapped me back to the presence of an almost empty waiting area, temporarily away from my gut eater.
"Here!" I had announced.
I got up and walked over. My hands quivered while they embraced each other. Suddenly, the hot weather had become more overbearing as my body heat rose.
"This way sir."
She led me into a little room in the back of the building. That scared the shit out of me and it showed in the tiny sweat beads that formed on my forehead. The door closed after we walked into the dense space of the room.
"Please have a seat," she had said.
Ms. Ann Demus, as it said on her id, held some papers in front of her; obviously they were information on me. I stared at her middle-aged, light skinned, freckled face. Her expression was emotionless while she leafed through quietly with manicured hands. I was tempted to ask her why she did not get all the details together before calling me in there to be a nervous wreck, but I contained myself.
"Your results are back."
"Well, no shit sherlock!"
The heat that I felt inside almost caused me to say my thought out loud.
"I need you to sign these papers for me."

She handed me the papers after putting an x by the places she wanted me to sign. I took them unwillingly with my patience running dry. Then as if she read my mind and was trying to stop the fury that would have been unleashed within the next minute, Ms. Demus spoke to me.
"Your results are negative Mr. De-Angelo."
My heart stopped ripping through my chest like an axe, my sweat dried up for a day of drought, and a smile reared its head on my face. I gladly fulfilled her request, thanked her and left.

The vibration that I suddenly felt at my side caused my reappearance from the memory that held me prisoner for a few minutes. The phone beamed 'unknown' on the screen. My first impulse told me to neglect the call, but I could not because I would not know if it was an emergency.
"Hello?"
"Chris, this is Brenda."
"Shit!" I cried softly.
Then my voice suddenly became crusty and hoarse.
"Oh Hi Brenda."
"What's up you sick or something?" she asked.
"Yeah. Don't feel too well, I have bad a cold."
I ignored her sexy tone, and the fact that she called me her lover.
"I can't reach you lately. What's up with that?"
"Let me call you back," I said quickly.
"I hope you're not playing games with me Chris. Every time I call I get your voice mail."
"I know. I've been busy. But I'll call you back."
Brenda hesitated then reluctantly gave in.
"Make sure you call me," she demanded.

"Um-umh," was all I could answer before hanging up the phone.

The thunderous headache that struck after I hung up the phone did much justice for Celine. My guilt ate at me all over and forced me into paralysis on my bed. Moments later I got up and prepared to meet Celine.

By ten thirty I was outside her door. My heart fought recklessly inside my chest as I contemplated running back to my car and getting as far away as my shameful self would allow me to go. But I knew that my luck had run out and it was time to be straight with her. I knew I had to face her, Celine deserved that much and even more. My finger hesitantly crept up on her buzzer, and applied pressure sounding my arrival. Then in what seemed like less than a second she was by the door greeting and ushering me inside.

"Hi, how are you?"

I felt so small after those words left my mouth.

"Ok. So let's get to the point here."

Celine gave me direct eye contact and their staying power rang the bell that told me she was not accepting anymore crappy excuses.

"Ok, what's up?" I asked.

At first I saw a bit of anger rise in her eyes and tensed body movements told me she wanted to just strangle me right then. But, as soon as it came, the look left and she resumed speaking to me calmly and rationally.

"I just really want to know what's up Chris. Why are you pulling away from me? Do you regret proposing to me? Because I would rather you take back the ring than let things go on this way between us."

"Oh baby, no way. I love you, and I would never have asked if I really did not want you to be my wife."

"So what's up then?" she pleaded.

There was pain in her voice and her eyes glossed with tears.

"I haven't really been feeling like myself much. The whole issue of opening up this new book store was a bit much. I did not really want to worry you with my frustrations of getting things done right."

"Sweetheart! I completely forgot about your new store. I'm sorry. But these are the things that couples lean on each other for."

"I know honey and I promise I will try not to shut you out again. I'm sorry."

She walked over and threw her arms over my shoulders. Her long, comforting embrace delivered the message that she really had missed me a lot and it had been difficult to deal with. Eventually, Celine's lips found mine, soft and teasing, then rubbing, then licking and sucking. Soon it was unable to tell whose tongue was whose as we devoured each other.

"I want to feel you inside me Chris," Celine purred.

She opened the buttons on my shirt one by one while kissing my face and neck. And I responded in the same fashion by ripping the T-shirt she wore over her head. I deeply inhaled her breasts into my mouth and delivered tender suction.

"Oh Chris, I want you so much."

"I want you too baby."

She was out of breath as she took my hand and guided it to her juice. I gently glided my index finger over her clitoris.

"Ahhh!"

Her screams were soft and sweet, yet loud and pleasing. She was so wet.

"Ohhh! I want you Chris! I want to feel all of you inside me."

The sound of her in ecstasy begging me to take her was enough for me to spin her around, throw her over the living room couch, and dive right in.

Her ass became flushed as if screaming out in its own pleasure with each satisfying motion.

"Ahhhh!"

We united in our mind blowing explosion. Afterwards, we caressed as new lovers that could not get enough of each other.

Celine

Our relationship was back on track again after our little talk last week. Still, I wondered whether Chris and I were doing the right thing by moving so fast. Already we were engaged to get married and Chris had not felt obligated enough to talk to me about his worries. My office phone beeped and took me out of my momentary trance.

"Celine, Mr. Miller's on line one."

"Thank you Ellen."

I picked up the phone and pressed the blinking button.

"Hi Rob, what's going on?"

"What's up babe? Just called to see how you're doing."

"Am good. Are you home?"

"Yeah, took the day off today."

"You ok?" I asked.

"Yeah, yeah, I'm fine. Just one of those days when you get up and feel like staying in bed."

"Oh, I know what you mean."

"So, Celine are we still on for tonight?" he asked.

A brief scan of my brain reminded me that I had agreed to accompany him to a barbeque that night.

"Yeah."

"Ok then, I'll see you at six thirty."

"See you later Rob."

"Bye."

Rob had been capturing more and more of my attention lately. At times I even found myself wondering if there could be more involved than what was on the surface. Oftentimes I would end up shaking off the feeling and dismissing it. My situation was just unclear to me. Chris and I had been getting along fine until he proposed. And Rob was a sweet person who was always there when I needed him.

I thought back to the previous night when Chris had come by. After we made up I felt so good inside. The sexual height that we attained again and again could not be explained. My sex drive had gone from mild to extreme since I met Chris. This made me wonder whether what we had was merely sexual.

Rob arrived to pick me up at six. He was dressed in a white muscle shirt, white Reeboks, and a black knee-length jeans shorts. For the occasion I wore a baby-blue wrap mini skirt, a white spaghetti strap tee, and white strap up slippers. I finished off with baby-blue decorative jewelry.

Rob introduced me to a few of his friends that were present. They had cooked up quite a storm; pork, chicken, sausages, burgers, fish, goat, oxtail, rice and beans, rolls, not to mention the variety of fruits, salads, and juices. I put a little of almost everything on my plate. Rob and I sat on two chair facing each other, and held the plates in our hands as we ate.

"Wow! Whoever cooked this food surely could open up a restaurant," I mentioned.

"Yes, Pat and her family really could cook. Everything always taste good."

"You know when sometimes you might enjoy one part of a meal and not the next? This is not the case at all because all this food taste good."

Rob and I chitchatted some more while we finished eating. He took my plate and emptied it when we were done.

"Would you like something else to drink?" he asked.

"I'll take some water, thanks."

I had been having some wine before. I knew that I got tipsy pretty fast so I decided not to have any more liquor. Rob came back and handed me an eight ounce bottle of Always Springs water.

"Thanks."

Just then Usher's voice blared through the speaker.

"Would you like to dance?"

I wanted to but I was shy. Besides, I did not know anyone else that was there.

"No, thanks."

"Ah, come on," Rob insisted.

He held on to my waist as we walked over. Beenie Man's voice blasted through the speakers while we began grinding on each other. I was having a good time and suddenly my uncertainty about my relationship with Chris seemed justified. Only time would tell my next move as I danced the night away with Rob.

Chris

I felt like it was time to come clean with Celine about my mistake with Brenda. My mind would not allow me to believe that she would walk out on me. After all, we were in the middle of planning our wedding. Celine knew I loved her just like I knew that she loved me. Surely, all it would do is prove to be one of our obstacles along the way. Besides, my honesty should count for something.

I had been calling both Celine's phones all day long but I was unable to get her. It was just my luck that as I got ready to come clean something got in the way. So instead, I went to shoot hoops with the boys. We had just finished playing and I stood in the locker room with Pete. I put my foot up on the black rectangular bench to tie the shoelaces to my black and white Reeboks. Pete stood a couple feet to my right just pulling his tee shirt over his head.

"So what's up with Brenda?" Pete asked.

"She whiling son. Thinks I'm into her because of the one night stand."

"Ah you done fucked up and got your ass into hot waters that's gonna be boiling soon."

"Thanks for the support."

"You know you my boy and all, but you should have known this is where things were headed."

"You're right, I was careless and irresponsible."

I had not even told Pete the most serious part yet. I knew that he had my back no matter what, but I really did not want him to know until I was sure. The only problem was that I did not know how I was ever going to be sure.

"How's Celine?"

"I'm not sure what she's thinking. But, she was starting to question whether I loved her and really wanted her to be my wife."

"What do you plan to do cuz?" he asked.

"Don't know. Think I should just tell her the truth and let it be a test for us, that's if she decides to stay."

Pete's eyes widened as if he could not believe what I was saying to him. I really felt like I was in a hole that no one could dig me out of.

"Are you losing it man?" he asked.

Pete put down the exercise bag from his hand and came over to me. With his right hand he gave me a brotherly pat on the shoulder.

"I understand your concern, but think about this carefully before you make a decision. And then be prepared for the consequences of any conclusion you come to. Am here for you man, all I'm saying is it's gonna hurt her deep and it won't be easy to get over. She might not ever want to see you again."

I knew my boy cared about me. We went too far back for him not to.

"Ok bro, I've got a headache now. I'll think about it later. Let's bounce."

He went back for his bag and threw it over his shoulder. Pete walked out the door and held it open for me to follow. I grabbed my bag also and we walked to our cars and headed in different directions.

As I took my exit off the expressway, I wondered again about the fact that I could not reach Celine earlier in the day. After two rings she picked up. Her voice sounded grainy like she had been sleeping.

"You ok?" I questioned.

"Yeah, just tired."

"Been trying to call you all evening, where you been?"

"Went to catch a movie after work. I had put my phone on vibrate and forgot to put it back on."

"I'm coming over, need to tell you something."

"Where are you now?" Celine asked.

"Just got off the expressway. Was going home 'cause I couldn't reach you. But I'm turning around."

"Alright, see you in a little while."

"Ok, bye."

Celine

I greeted him with a hug and a kiss, which he gladly accepted, and then surprised me with a bunch of flowers consisting of beautiful white lilies and pink roses.

"Hi honey!"

"Hi my sweet."

"What's all this?" I asked.

"Missed you that's all."

Chris came in and followed me to the living room. I fetched a vase, went in the kitchen to get water, put the flowers in, and went back to the living room. I sat the vase now full of life on my center table, then sat beside Chris on the couch.

"So how's everything?" he asked.

"Fine. What have you been up to?"

"Just came from the gym with Pete. How was the movie?"

"It was pretty good."

"Who'd you go with?"

"Rob. He's a friend of mine from high school. We ran into each other the other day."

"When's the other day?"

"I don't remember. What's this an interrogation?"

I felt like I was being put on the spot for a crime I did not commit.

"No honey. I'm sorry."

Chris looked like he wanted to say more, but for reasons decided not to, which I was glad for because I really did not want to get into that. Besides, there was nothing going on between me and Rob but good friendship.

"Don't you have something to tell me?" I asked.

"Huh?"

Chris stared at me in total lost.

"You Said you had something to tell me," I reminded.

"I love you."

"That's it?"

"Yeah, was missing you and just wanted to tell you that."

"Ok."

I sensed that something else might have been bothering him, but just left things the way they were. Eventually, I knew that it would surface, whatever it was.

Sheria

The small, black clock on my dresser began to dance and vibrate.

"Oh shit, I need to get out of here!"

Being that I was so forgetful sometimes, I had set the clock to remind me of my doctor's appointment. Luckily, it was an hour ahead so I still had time to ready myself. I quickly got up and rushed towards the bathroom. Traffic was unpredictable and I really did not want to be late and end up having to be rescheduled as usual was the case.

"Oh shit! Ahhh!"

I jammed my foot into the bathroom door. A red blood shot instantly appeared on my big toe as the excruciating pain caused my toe to throb. I had to sit for a few minutes and allow the pain to wear off before showering.

One forty marked my arrival at the office, ten minutes later than my appointment schedule. There were as usual many clients waiting to see their respective doctors. I walked up to the counter and greeted the short, slender, glasses wearing, woman who sat behind it.

"Good afternoon, I have an appointment with Dr. Peterson."

"What time is your appointment?"

"One thirty."

The wrinkled face older brunette looked at the clock behind her before she reproved me for being late. She then unenthusiastically checked off my name and told me to have a seat. I scanned the sheet and mentally noted that there were two people checked ahead of me to see my doctor. I thought to myself 'the usual the way they always scheduled an appointment, but we don't get to actually see the doctor till an hour or so later'.

By the time I got out it was about three thirty-five. I felt exhausted and was on my way home to relax.
"Beep, beep, beep!"
My vibrator went off with sounds alerting me of a text message. My thumb clicked the "yes" button to read mail and the message displayed:
"Hi Sher! Do you want to go clubbing later, around eleven. Let me know, later!"
I smiled at the little smiley face that he stuck at the end of the message. I quickly wrote something back and hit the reply button at the stoplight before the green light transformed again.

<u>Chris</u>

I had not slept a wink last night. After Celine told me that she was going to hang with Sheria, I decided to stay home to try to clear my mind and stay out of trouble. It was no use, however, because trouble came looking for me. An hour had passed before I realized that I was upsetting my brain over the inevitable. So I jumped up and went to set the tub to take a cozy, quiet bubble bath. I turned my house phone ringers off and put my cell on vibrate.

"Solace and peace tonight. And I shall enjoy!" I said to myself.

After a refreshing and relaxing bath, I went in my bedroom, creamed my skin and got dressed in a pair of red and black silk boxer shorts. I got the chicken vegetable fried rice with shrimps that I had ordered before going in the bath, and relaxed on my living room couch. I fell in a comfort zone as channel after channel flashed by on the television screen. Being that I had an un-scrambler all the channels were available to me at all times. I put down the remote control on the couch beside me and decided to watch *Basic* with Samuel L. Jackson and John Travolta, a DVD I had seen twice before.

While curiosity and interest held my attention to the television, I was interrupted by the suddenly annoying sound of my doorbell. The thought that it could have been Celine made the pace of my footsteps speed up as excitement filled me. On reaching the door I was about to fling it open when a fuse in my mind warned me to be cautious. And it was a damn good thing I listened. Before my hand closed the one-inch gap between it and the doorknob, I withdrew and carefully peeked through the hole in the center of my door.

"*Damn! What the hell is she doing here?*"

That was all I could mutter through the rage that had suddenly erupted inside of me. On the other side of the door Brenda desperately tried to see through the hole as she continuously and stubbornly rang my bell over and over again. She probably thought I was really there and ignoring her, which was really the case, because my car was parked right outside. I decided to wait her out and see just how long she intended to ring my bell before she left.

After what seemed like eternity I saw the back of her head, then her full shapely figure, bumper and all, as she walked away seemingly disappointed.

"*I wonder what she wanted.*"

I questioned in vain as I had no reply for myself. But the bigger question that remained stuck in my mind was what the next step for Celine and I would be, especially after Brenda.

Celine

The camomile tea was so soothing as I laid in deep cleansing soapy bubbles. After downing the last bit of it I laid back with my head propped on the wall and closed my eyes. Once I started creeping up on the nice comfort of sleep my phone rang. On the third ring, eyes still closed, I reach for my cordless and pressed the talk button .

"Hello?" I answered.

"Honey you ok? Sound hoarse."

"Do I sound that bad?" I asked.

"I sense you had lots of fun last night," Chris noted.

"Yeah, a little too much fun," I replied.

"What are you doing today?"

"No plans yet. Have something in mind?" I asked.

"I want to see you, but my car is not working," Chris said.

"What's wrong with it?" I asked.

"I'm not sure. It's been making some funny noises so I took it to the shop. You want to drive by?"

"I don't really feel like driving today."

"Let's see...Up for the train?" he asked.

"The train? I don't really know my way around by train too much, but that'll be fine, I guess."

"I know. Once you get used to driving, nothing can compare."

"Where would we meet?" I asked.

"Let me see, I think uptown at Forty-second Street is a good spot. It should be easy for you to find."
"What time?"
"About the next two hours. Is that good for you?"
"I'm bathing so I could be ready to leave in like the next half hour."
"So you're buck naked right now?" Chris asked, with his voice teasing my ear.
"Yes, I'm buck naked right now. But we're talking about meeting here, hellooo."
We both slipped out a little laugh.
"No naughty business right now. I'll be ready to leave in a half an hour," I continued.
He was so funny sometimes and I loved him so much.
"So are you still naked?"
"Yes Chris, I'm still naked."
"Damn!"
"What's wrong?"
"Wish I was there so bad."
"You are just crazy. I thought something happened to you."
I smiled to myself knowing exactly what he was thinking.
"What would happen if you were here?" I asked.
"We would do the dooky doo."
A volcanic laughter exploded from my lips.
"Where'd you get that phrase from?" I asked.
Chris laughed on the other side of the line asking me not to tell anyone that such a thing came out of his mouth.
"I promise not to, it's toooo silly. Keep your cell phone close by ok?"

"I'll put the volume on high so I could hear you," I assured him.
"Alright then, I'll see you later."
"Ok my sweet see you later."

Chris

It happened at five p.m. in the middle of our train ride. We had found each other easily even though Celine had gotten there ten minutes earlier than I did. We met, walked around 42nd street for a little, and then Celine made a suggestion that led to confusion.

"Hey, we could go to Bowling Green and take a ride in the ferry," she suggested.

"Ok, fine with me. But let's grab something to eat first."

"There's a McDonald's right across the street about two blocks down."

"Ok."

We both got a veggie burger meal and orange drink.

"This burger is slammin'," Chris said.

"I know, the first time I tasted it I went to heaven," I agreed.

It took us about twenty-five minutes to finish up and get back to the train station. We got on the number four express train and sat next to each other in a corner two seater.

"Excuse me ladies and gentlemen, is there anyone who could help me to get some food?"

This man looked to be in his mid thirties with nappy hair and clean looking skin. The limp seemingly in his left foot was supported by a cane as he walked along constantly repeating himself. He wore a nice clean blue shirt with red jeans pants cut off at the knees, and was bare footed. Some people on the train ignored him, others even gave him dirty looks as he moved along. Celine quickly shuffled through her purse and took out a five-dollar bill.

"Here sir."

"Thank you miss, thank you. Thanks so much, God bless you."

Joy danced in the man's eyes as if he had just won the lottery. He exited through the side door to our car and went in the next to carry on his journey. Just then the train stopped at Brooklyn Bridge and exactly as the automated voice gave warning that the doors were about to close, a woman ran in almost getting caught between. She looked up, I noticed her face more clearly, and froze in my skin.

Celine

"Chris."

It was an exclamation as well as a question in her tone as she called his name. The lady that busted through the train doors just moments earlier took the four footsteps that separated her from us. I found it peculiar that he did not answer her, did not even look up.

"It *is* you. What's up?" the woman asked.

Chris's head slowly rose and then as if his worse nightmare had come through his face instantly reddened. With the expression of a child being scolded by his mother he barely muttered while looking passed her.

"Hi."

"Who's the friend?" she asked.

The woman had a heavy hood voice and smiled as she spoke. I stared at the tightness of the blue pum-pum shorts that she wore and her tits that popped out of the white tube top that matched her shoes and handbag. Chris hesitated before introducing me.

"Celine, Brenda. Brenda, Celine."

It was so quick and lifeless I barely heard the pronunciation of her name right.

"Hi Brenda, nice to meet you," I offered with an outstretched palm.

I tried to be polite although I did not know the woman, and wished that she had not broken up the special moment between me and Chris. The woman refused my hand, and the smile she wore moments earlier no longer danced on her reddened lips.

"Hi Shelby."

She had the nerve to call me by the wrong name then rudely turn back her attention to Chris after she rolled her eyes.

"So when you coming by?" Brenda asked.

"I'll talk with you later," he said.

"Why we can't talk now? I came by your house, and I called you, but you haven't been answering."

"Later ok?"

Chris's eyes pleaded with her desperately to understand that the moment was just not right.

"She don't know, does she?" the woman asked.

All this time I had been sitting there trying to understand what the heck was going on. Different things ran through my mind, but I wanted to wait to hear what was really up before jumping the gun. But her comment really piqued my curiosity and even some anger.

"Know what?" I demanded.

I made no attempt to hide the annoyance in my voice.

"Figures," she looked mad, "Can't get out of this Chris. You have to own up to your responsibility."

"Chris, what the heck is going on, and who is this woman?"

At this point eyes from everywhere pierced the three of us and tried to scan our brains to try to get the full details of what was really going on.

"Calm down Celine, we'll talk later."

My head started to drum as anger flamed inside me.

"She deserves to know Chris," Brenda emphasized.

Hearing this woman's voice again pissed me off even more and it became unbearable.

"Somebody please tell me what the heck is going on."

"I'm his baby momma," she announced full of pride.

I laughed nervously.

"Baby momma? Chris don't have any kids."

"Yes he does, ask him."

"Chris?"

I looked over at him knowing damn well that this man of mine was different from the rest of them. My last emotion to flow through my mind got stuck and no matter how hard I tried to kick it out, it just would not move. My mind knew better than my heart.

"Chris?"

I tried desperately to hold my ground and not show any sign of weakness. As Chris spoke, his head remained turned and his eyes were not visible to me.

"I just found out a few weeks ago."

The why was somewhere in my head but would not roll off my tongue. I slowly got up and stood by the door. When the train stopped at Wall Street I got off unsure of where I was going. All I knew was that I was confused in the head and hurt in the heart.

Chris

My heart wanted so much to go after Celine the day before, but I knew it was best at the time to let her go. Celine got off the train and I de-bounded the stop after with Brenda in tow.

"Why the hell are you still following me?" I barked.

"She had to know."

"It was not your position to tell her. I was going to let her know at the right time."

"If she loves you she'll forgive you, and accept your son too."

"You don't know anything about her so shut the hell up, ok."

"Don't you get all angry with me, it's not my fault."

"I'll talk with you soon concerning our son just not now."

"Your son will be here in a couple of months so get over it fast and deal with reality."

As she walked off I stared at the woman who in just one night ruined my life in such a major way. I contemplated not telling Celine that the worse part was that I had slept with Brenda, but was unsure if that was the right choice.

I touched the side of my head and staggered a bit from after effects of the sleeping medicine I had downed last night. I had gotten home eventually, still wrecked in the head and unable to shake insomnia. Thinking beers were my best remedy I went to the refrigerator, and after about six bottles of Heinekens I passed out. Even after awaking the next day my mind constantly kept me on thoughts of Celine. The ring of my phone echoed through.

"Hello baby, I'm so glad you called."

"Man, last time I checked I was straight, and my ass was not your baby."

My voice sank for the first time hearing my best friend's voice.

"I'm going through hell man," I admitted.

"What happened bro? You sound like shit."

His deep concern for me was usual, but I knew there was nothing he was able to do to help get me out of my mess.

"She found out."

"Who found what out?" Pete asked.

"Celine. She found out about Brenda."

"How?"

"Yesterday I was on the train going to Bowling Green with Celine, when Brenda popped up on the train and blew shit out of proportion."

"What did she say?" he asked.

"She told Celine about the kid."

"Hold up! What kid?"

In my sorrowful stage I had completely forgotten that I had not mentioned that part to Pete before. I knew that he would be crushed finding out that way, but it was too late because I had already slipped.

"Uh...," I stuttered.

"Yeah, let me hear this fucked-up drama now."

"Well, I didn't want to tell you because I'm not sure, but Brenda has a child that she says is mine."

"Oh boy!" Pete sighed, "you need to get as far away from that skank as possible. Especially, if you plan on keeping Celine."

"I gotto at least find out man. Don't want to have a bastard child running around out there."

"You talking all this crap after five fucking years? That bitch ran off with no remorse and now she comes running back and you're putting up with her bullshit?"

I knew that things would have been that intense when I told Pete the whole story. He knew that I really loved Brenda and would have given her all that I had just to make her happy. Pete saw how much it broke me down after she left. All I could do at that point was to just remain silent and allow him to unleash his thoughts.

"You know what? Fuck Brenda! Don't want to hear anymore about her."

More silence clouded our telephone conversation before Pete broke it.

"Have you spoken to Celine?"

"No. I keep calling, but she won't answer. She's the best thing that has happened to me for a while, and I don't know how to deal with this son. I don't want to lose her."

"Don't know what to tell you bro. Just hope everything works out for you."

"She was really hurt about me lying to her."

"You'll figure this out."

"I hope so."

"Ms. Thang is beeping in on the next line..."

"Aight, we'll talk later."

I hung up and took the phone back off the hook in one motion.

"Hi, this is Celine. Please leave me a brief message with your name and number and I'll get back to you, bye."

I kept hitting redial and still got the same message that had become annoying. After I realized that I could not really blame her for being upset, I finally left a message.

Celine

I looked in the mirror and saw the reflection of a torn woman. Swollen eyes, and a pale face matched my feelings of betrayal and pain. After leaving Sheria's apartment last night I felt better. But as soon as I reached home the tears began to flow again. In the morning as I looked at my reflection in the mirror I concluded that I could not make it in to work. I did not want the visibility of my tremulous personal life to be bomb-blasted around the office.

By evening I was still a wreck. Tons of messages bombarded my answering machine, so I pressed the play button and listened. During the first seven or so calls the person hung up and then Chris' voice registered through my head.

Beep ..."Hey Celine. Baby we need to talk. I know that I should have told you the instant I found out and I'm sorry I didn't. Please call me and let's talk about this. I love you. Bye."

I was unsure of what I was most upset about. The fact that he lied by withholding the truth or that some ill-mannered skank had his first born child, something that I could never replace. I knew I had to call him but I did not want to.

Beep ..."Celine, it's mom. Your dad and I are just checking in, give us a call. Love you honey."

After I listened to all my messages I turned off my answering machine. I went to the refrigerator and got some ice cream. I took it up to my room, put in my old episodes of 'Friends', and stuffed my face.

Sheria

When I first saw her I knew instantly the type of person that she was. I could tell that she was an avid clubber who took much pride in her skimpy attires. And sure enough as I had her followed, all the spots that she regularized were party spots. I had waited for the opportune time to acquaint myself with Brenda. I knew that eventually the right time would approach. And the right time was then so I began the initial stage of my master plan to befriend her. I had followed Brenda to K-Mart and strolled around in good distance behind her. With an empty handcart I decided to cease the moment.

"Excuse me, can I please see that gel in your shopping cart?" I asked.

"Sure."

I took the round, blue jar from her hand adorned with colorful nails at least two inches long.

"Someone had recommended it to me but I never came across it anywhere," I lied.

"Yeah, it's pretty good for all hair types. Plus it is non-greasy and does not get hard and flaky like the others."

"Oh really?" I faked enthusiasm.

"Huh-uh, that's why I always buy it."

"Where did you pick it up?" I asked her.

"Oh, it's in isle seven."

She pointed towards her right.

"Thanks. By the way where did you get your color done?"

"Actually, a friend of mine did it. She's currently in the process of opening her own salon so she welcomes new clients. I'll give you her number if you like so you can call and set up an appointment."

"Ok. You can give me your number too just in case."

"Alright."

Brenda handed me the piece of white paper that she jotted down the numbers on.

"Thanks."

"You're welcome."

I smiled at her and turned in the opposite direction. Brenda had met my acquaintance and my plan was off to a start. As I walked out of the supermarket empty-handed I felt my phone vibrate against my waist. I saw the funny face smiling on the caller's id before I answered.

"What up beau?" I answered.

"Nada. Where you at?"

"On my way home, why?"

"Was just wondering if you wanted to go shopping or something."

"Well sure. I'm always up for spending mullah," I said in a teasing voice while laughing.

"Girl you a trip. Just be quiet and come straight here," Celine said.

"Ok mamma, bye."

I smiled as I thought of my gratefulness for having such a wonderful friendship with Celine. When I got there twenty-five minutes later she was already at the door looking anxious and impatient. In no time she sat next to me in the passenger side of my car.

"Hey sis!" she greeted.

"Hey girl!"

"I had begun reading a novel that Chris gave me, but even that did not help too much. I was just so bored out of my mind, and when I'm bored I think too damn much for my own good."

"And what's so bad about thinking?" I asked.

"Too many thoughts of this kid situation is racking my mind. I thought I would be able to handle it, but I am very uncomfortable."

"Why is that?"

"I don't know."

Silence conquered the atmosphere and then she continued.

"It's not like the child existed before, you know? He just literally popped up outta nowhere, and suddenly I have to deal with a step child, *and* a baby mamma."

"I think you're worried over nothing. Chris is not even sure that the child is his yet."

"You don't think the child is his? Why would she do such a thing if it weren't? That would be pure evil."

"All I'm saying is don't get so worked up when nothing is for sure. Ask Chris to take a paternity test."

"Are you insane? I can't do that," Celine protested.

"And why not? It's your life too. You deserve that much and even more for being stuck in the middle."

"Maybe you're right, but don't you think that he should think of that himself. Then again he probably won't because he's so damn sensitive."

"Well, you have to protect your feelings also. You need to be sure, and as matter of fact so does he."

"I guess I have homework for tonight. Enough about me, what's up with you these days?" Celine asked.

"You know it's always the same old things going on. My life is a bore, and there haven't been much sex lately."

"Really? Have you ran out of unfamiliar people to sex up already?"

Celine played it off so wonderfully with her enlarged eyes complementing the surprise in her voice, and the rest of her body language. I squinted my eyes, shook my head and made a funny face.

"Shut up!"

I smiled and Celine laughed out. She always had jokes about my 'so active' sex life as she called it.

What about that girl you screwed the other day?" she asked.

"Oh come on Celine, you know I'm not gay. I just swing to the other side every now and then for a taste of something different," I boasted.

She shook her head and laughed.

"Why you laughing? You know it's the truth."

"You a trip and a half when it comes to that one. You need to be careful of diseases and all that shit."

"I *am* girl, don't worry."

I pulled up in the parking lot of Brooklyn Mall. As soon as we hit the entrance, the attack of the racks began with a vengeance.

Celine

My tears had come and gone. I was ready to at least try to give Chris and I a chance regardless of the circumstance. I had ignored him the whole time and the guilt I felt from letting go of what we had only got stronger. I really loved him and had to admit that we were pretty good together. My finger traced the frame that held a five by seven photo of us on my desk.

"*I miss you baby,*" I whispered wishing that things were different between us.

He had called day and night, but I was unable to get up enough nerve to answer. I decided that it was time for me to call him. My right index finger reached forward and pressed the speaker button before dialing his cell number. On the first ring he picked up.

"Hi my sweet!"

"We need to talk. Can you meet me after work?"

"Sure! Where do you want to meet?" he asked.

"Downtown by that new store we went to a few weeks ago."

"On 6th and Forty-second?" he verified.

"Yeah, I leave work at four today."

"Alright then see you later."

"Ok, bye."

I was really supposed to leave at five. But after hearing his sexy baritone voice and visualizing his delicious full lips sucking on mine I knew that I would not make it until then. I dialed Ellen's extension.

"Hi Celine."

"Ellen, I'll be leaving at four today."

"Ok."

"Thanks."

Afterwards I sat there thinking about what I would say to Chris. But I knew the words would come just the way they were meant to.

I got up and paced around the large space in my office. I surrounded myself with dear memories of all that I loved. I had a painting on the wall that my mom had given me for my twenty-first birthday. It displayed an older woman and a younger version of the woman, whom I assumed to be her daughter. The two were parting, yet neither one wanted to let go. I smiled because she could not have given me a better painting. My eyes wandered again and next caught the attention of a picture of Chris is his boxer short posing like superman. Once again I smiled because those indeed were happy moments.

I sat by my desk and began to clean up in preparation to leave the office.

Sheria

A broad smile shined on my face while I sealed the envelope and dropped it off at the post office. The one hundred dollars that was exchanged for the paper would prove to be well worth it in a few days. My instincts turned out to be right so my reason for getting acquainted with Brenda was worth it after all. I walked back outside and jumped in my car.

"So what exit did you say we need to take?" I asked.

"Take, ah Linden Boulevard. She lives on Pennsylvania Avenue."

I had picked up Brenda minutes earlier and we were now on our way to get our hair done. We had definitely become closer in the past few weeks. She seemed a bit lazy and preferred things to be handed to her, but aside from that she was a pretty cool person.

The weather was a not so bad fifty-six degrees outside. We got to Pam's house and after a difficult time finding parking, Brenda and I finally went inside. Her house was huge and well cared for from what I saw.

"Hi," Pam greeted.

"Hello," I replied.

"Please excuse the messy appearance. I am renovating and currently installations are being done."

"When did you become so polite heifer?" asked Brenda.

"Well excuse you, but I do know how to separate business from pleasure."

From the looks of it this Pam person seemed to have a feisty personality, which would explain why she and Brenda were long time friends to begin with.

"Whateva," Brenda replied with a wave of her hand.

I sat in a white plastic chair. As I watched Brenda and Pam I thought of Celine. Those kinds of friendships were just too weird among females and whenever I encountered people with such bond I always felt good inside.

"So ahh..."

Pam looked in my direction. I figured that she had forgotten my name.

"Sheria, it's Sheria," I reminded her.

"Yes, Sheria. What are you getting today."

"I would like that color Brenda has in a layered shoulder length cut."

"Ok could do. Do you need a treatment?"

"Sure, might as well."

"Alright."

Pam reached in a cupboard and retrieved some bottles and containers. I watched as she mixed a creamy solution, laid out all her equipment, and put on her gloves. She came over and started rummaging through my hair before beginning to apply the mixture.

"So, what area are you from Sheria?" she asked.

"I live in Cypress Hills."

"Really? I have a cousin who lives over in that area. We don't see each other much though."

Pam went over to the cupboards again and brought another towel.

"And how's Robert, Brenda?"

"Up to no good as usual. I'm trying to cut him the heck off."

"How do you intend to do that when he always has to come around?" Pam asked.

Brenda shifted in her seat.

"Let's not go there," she said.

I could tell from the way that Brenda responded that there was something she did not want me to know. They abruptly stopped the conversation and we sat in quiet for a while until we started talking about the latest news about the ongoing war in Iraq.

Chris

I had just gotten home from the gym and was about to go inside when I spotted an overflow in my mailbox. I walked over to retrieve them and that was when I spotted the bright, peach colored envelop. On my way inside I ripped the paper as my curiosity controlled me. I carefully pulled out and unfolded an eight by eleven piece of white paper. My interest caused me to stop midway my tracks to read the paper and sort out its message in my mind. There were no formalities, no return address, nothing but the disturbing information within. I finished the few steps towards my coach and gave in to my weakened knees. I sat there trying to figure out my thoughts, but I was unsure of what they really were at that point. A few more minutes passed and then something snapped in my head and I wanted answers. I grabbed my keys and went right back out the door.

My boisterous arrival perhaps caused neighbors to stir as I knocked on her door being that the dilapidated bell was broken. Moments later I heard footsteps lazily approach the door.

"Who is it?" she asked with sleep still apparent in her voice.

Obviously, she had no way of telling who was at her door being that there were no apparent peepholes, unless her side of the door was transparent. Anyway, I still decided to answer because she would gladly open up for me at any time.

"It's me, Chris."

Within seconds the door flew open and her nakedness shined through the soft, thin, yellow robe that she wore.

"Hi. What are you doing here so early?"

Pete and I had decided to hit the gym early that Saturday morning and so by that time it was about 9 a.m. Her smile was devious and naughty as Brenda stepped towards me expecting an embrace. I stepped back with palms in front of me to ward her off.

"I only came here for one thing and it's not sex, so get the thought out of your head."

"What is it you came for then?"

Her facial expression showed confusion.

"Can I come in?"

Brenda hesitated and got deep in thoughts as if she wanted to ask me to leave. But the look on my face must have told her that I would come in by force regardless so she might as well had stepped aside and let me in.

"Ok but only for a little while because I'm really tired."

I marched inside and immediately wished I had not as the stench of her apartment made its way up my nostrils. I wanted to stand, but in order not to make her feel uncomfortable I decided to sit just on the edge of her chair.

"So what's this about?"

"Where's your son?" I asked.

"Why you asking? I told you he was with my parents."

"Where's that?" I inquired some more.

"In Atlanta, why?"

"Am I his father?"

A look of shock crossed her face and tears threatened to erupt.

"How could you ask me such a question? I already told you he is your son."

"Don't lie to me Brenda! This has gone far enough, ever as far as threatened to destroy my relationship."

There was apparent anger in my voice, which perhaps scared her because her facial expression turned to one of concern.

"Why you asking all these questions, Chris?"

Her lowered tone was rhetorical. I took out the paper that I had neatly folded and placed in my back pocket, and handed it to her. Her hands trembled as she took the paper and unfolded it.

"What's this?" she asked.

"You tell me Brenda. What *is* it?"

She hesitated as though she was thinking what to say next. Looking at me she could tell that I was not about to back down.

"You come around after five years and turn my life upside down and I'm just suppose to sit by and watch? Hell nah, I want to know the truth! Who's Robert Dailey?" I demanded.

Tears welled in her eyes before falling down her reddened cheeks. She allowed the birth certificate to glide away from her hand and fall to the ground.

"Why did you lie to me?" I shouted.

Brenda's chin rested on her neck bone and she remained silent.

"Now I'm so glad you left years ago because I would have never wanted a liar for a wife.

"I'm sorry Chris, please forgive me."

"You almost ruined my life all because of a dumb ass lie."

"You don't understand."

"What the fuck is there to understand? You know what? I'm outta here don't even answer."

With that I slammed her door behind me and went back to the car feeling very perturbed.

Celine

I was elated at the thought that it was all a lie. While I was upset that Brenda would have done such a horrible thing, the bottom line was he was all mine again. Therefore, Chris and I was out to celebrate.

"This steak tastes wonderful, honey," I commented.

I opened my mouth and allowed Chris to put another fork full of food in. He took up another piece of meat this time with his thumb and forefinger. My tongue invited his finger and licked all the steak juices.

"Mmmm! Baby you're turning me on," he complained with a teasing, sexy voice.

I gave him my best bedroom eyes and sucked more seductively.

"Oh Chris stop it," I purred.

"My Charlie is hard baby."

"As always," I said.

"Only for you my sweet."

"Let me see it."

I moved closer to him without being too suspicious. All around us other lovers and perhaps some friends ate happily in the prestigious restaurant. Nobody was watching and so I proceeded to reach my hand underneath the table. And as sure as winter will come and New York will get cold, Chris's rod stood still like a soldier in training. I was starting to get aroused myself as I zipped his fly and allowed my right hand to find the bare skin.

"I want you inside of me," I whispered in his ear.

My thoughts and openness surprised even me. But I felt like nothing much else mattered because we were in love.

"Don't torture me baby," he begged.

"I'm not. Meet me in the men's bathroom in two minutes."

With that I got up and swayed my behind away from our table. I had no idea where the courage came from, but I knew it was already built and I was not about to half-step. When Chris came in he met me bent over with my legs spread apart. The emotion that came over me from the sight of his constricted desires could hardly be explained.

"You're so nasty," Chris acknowledged.

"Thank you."

"Welcome."

His grin was as wide as my open spot. Within minutes he was behind me half naked. There were no obstacles since I had taken off my g-string and hiked my skirt around my waist.

"You feel so good," he commented.

"Ahh, yeah baby right there, that's my spot. Don't...Stop."

"You like that?" Chris asked.

My breathing got even heavier as I felt him swell some more inside of me.

"Ye...ah, I like...it."

Within minutes we were done, had cleaned ourselves and were ready to leave. Still glowing from our sex we just opened the door as though we were in our own private spot. A man and seemingly his woman stood on the other side. She stood with her eyes bulging, and her mouth formed an O. The man, however, had a devilish smirk on his face. I figured that the couple must have been on their way out when he wanted to use the bathroom and so she followed him. Then he must have heard our love sounds and decided to be voyeuristic. Chris's and I stood for a few seconds shocked at the idea of being caught. Then, in an instant being caught did not matter to me anymore.

"Excuse us."

With Chris hand in mine, I strutted passed them feeling like a bad ass kid, yet shameless.

Sheria

I sat home thinking about the big circle of life. It was five o'clock on a cold Thursday evening. I had stayed home from work because I had a major headache that morning and could hardly move without the jabs becoming more intense. I ended up sleeping for most of the day so by the time I got up I was like an energized bunny being driven by Duracel batteries. Brenda crossed my mind because we had become so close in the few weeks that we had known each other. Her carefree attitude made her likable to me, and she also kept me laughing all the time with her weird jokes. However, sometimes I saw despair in her eyes way beyond the smile that stays on the surface of her face.

...Ring!

I reached over to pick up the phone.

"Hello?"

"Hi girl, what's up?"

"Hey Celine. Just leaving work?"

"Yeah, I'm coming over for a little."

"Great! Can you get me a Snicker's bar on your way? Miss Red is in town."

Celine laughed knowing what I meant. My menstrual was in progress and forever caused me to crave chocolate. That damned Snicker's bar especially, always did something for me.

"Sure, I'll see you in a bit."

I would do anything for Celine, just as she would for me. I loved her so much and she did such a good job at being the sister that I never had. I got up and went to the kitchen to make her some fruit juice. She just loved her some freshly made fruits chopped and blended with minimum amount of water and sugar. The funniest thing about that was she would not make it herself; she only loved the way I did it.

We hugged and gave each other our usual cheek kisses before she came inside.

"Made you some fruit juice," I stated like an overjoyed little kid.

"Oh sweetie, you're such a darling."

"Thanks, I know."

Celine proceeded to the kitchen after taking off her boots at the door.

"You look hot today. Have a date?" I asked.

"Nah, I'm always looking hot. Besides, gotta keep the flames in my fiery relationship sizzling, you know?"

I laughed and Celine did also. There was something different about her lately. She seemed more vivacious and I was more than thrilled to see her in that mood.

She wore a gray and black wool, five inches above the knee length skirt with a black turtleneck sweater and thick, matching stockings.

"So what's up? I asked her while she helped herself to some juice.

"*Nada*. Came to check on my girl. You weren't at work today so I decided to stop by to see what's up. Make sure there's nothing serious going on over here 'cause I couldn't stand something being wrong with you."

"Ohh! You make me wanna cry. Look at you getting all emotional," I teased.

"Whatever girl. Anyway, what's really up with you?" Celine asked.

"Really?"

"Yeah really, why would I ask?"

"Are you sure you *really, really* want to know? I have to make sure."

"Girl get with it please," she said.

"I've got to tell you that this is really deep."

"When was I ever not able to handle deep? Now start yabbing before I have to find a cat for you."

"You're so evil! You know I'm scared of those furry little beasts."

"I know and I hope you remember some time soon and stop playing with me before I have to play Mrs. Dr. Evil."

"Alright here it is, ahhh, I, I just had an headache and so I had to stay home."

I smiled knowing that she was expecting something much more serious.

"Stop kidding me Sher, there's a time and place for everything under the sun."

"I'm serious sweetie. No matter what I tell you you still expect more. Stop worrying Celine, everything's ok."

"You're such a horrible person for doing this to me," she joked.

"Thanks, I've been practicing."

We both laughed while we made our way back to the living room.

"Alright girl, we gonna hang out this weekend. Call me," she said.

"You leaving already?" I asked.

I already settled in to enjoying her company, especially since I had been home alone the whole day.

"Yeah, promised Rob I'd meet him downtown."

"You still seeing that loser?"

"He's not a looser, and we're just friends."

"Well, I suggest you think about what's more important, your *'friend'* Rob or your *fiancé* Chris. I know for a fact that he would never approve, and if the situation were turned you would not want to hear it either."

A short period of silence rung through. I was determined in my mind to get Celine to leave that Rob guy alone. Besides, I always thought that he was creepy even though I had never met him. Ever since she announced that they were dating back in high school I always got the shivers when I thought of him. The day she told me that they parted, I had my own secret celebration.

"It's not just you anymore you're in a relationship and the next person should count. Just think about it," I insisted.

"Alright, if you promise to get off my back I'll think about it. People would think you're Chris's best friend and not mine."

"I am *your* best friend and that is why I am saying this to *you*."

"Ok enough! Let me get out of here already."

"Call me later."

"Ok, bye."

Even as I locked the door behind Celine I felt worried about her. The relationship that she had with that Rob whoever just did not sit right with me at all. I hoped that she would really think about what I had said to her and stop seeing him.

Chris

The fifth of June. That was the date set for our special day. I was just as ecstatic or perhaps even more excited than Celine about our joyous intended union. It had been a horrendous battle getting her to relinquish the management of the location. I wanted to surprise her and also be involved each step of the way, so I pressed until she eventually gave in. It was my special day also, contrary to the wide belief that only women get anxious about their weddings.

Anyway, I had found the perfect spot and could hardly wait to see the look on her face when she saw it. One condition of her agreeing to allow me to take care of that part of our wedding was that Sheria be involved in all the steps of my planning and whatever opinion she gave had to be taken into consideration. Therefore, most of the times whatever I was doing Sheria was there or I had to keep her updated on what was going on.

I was on my way to the gym. Being that I had missed the pass two days with Pete I called him up earlier to see if he wanted to swing. As I was about to get out of my car I saw Pete pull up in the empty parking space beside me.

"Hey stranger, 'sup?" I called out after he turned down the volume of Fifty Cent's voice on his speakers.

"What's going on bro?" Pete greeted.

We gave each other our special pound and pulled in for a halfway hug.

"I see married life have already taken you away from me," he said.

"Nah son, never that. You still my boy, just been a bit busy trying to make our wedding a unique one for my beau."

"So how's it going?"

"Not too bad. I'm really excited, but I still have doubts man. Feel like I should tell Celine about Brenda before we move on. I just think we should be able to get passed it you know?"

"Don't know what to tell you man. That's a tough cookie if there ever was one. All I can say is, think carefully and I hope things work out for the best."

"I could just leave it behind me, but you know how that saying goes. 'The past always comes back to haunt you'."

We said that phrase together because two of our boys got caught up in that situation before, so we knew the effect.

"I couldn't stand losing her. She's the best thing that has happened in my life since I can remember and I really love her."

"I know you do, but we don't control everything. Whatever you decide think about the long-term consequences. Whatever was meant will be so don't worry so much."

"Wish it was that easy. I swear my brain have a mind of its own."

He smiled, "I feel the same way sometimes."

Pete came over and supported me while I lifted some weights lying back on the bench. Then I did the same for him before we went to do some crunch and other exercise techniques.

Celine

I had just returned home from another visit to Eden Bridals. I returned once more empty-handed because I was unable to decide on one from among all the beautiful dresses. The next time had to be it though, as I had to promise Sheria because we had gone back and forth too many times before. I got inside, turned on the light, and was greeted with the ton loads of bills I had been avoiding for the last two days. I decided to sort through them this time and stop my procrastination. My cell phone bill came up to sixty dollars and eight cents, which was the usual price range. I picked up another and immediately tossed it; just more creditors wanting me to sign up with them. I had enough credit cards and was not even trying to get any more. The fifth envelope I picked up was the color of a ripe banana.

"What could this be?" I wondered.

I could not even determine the sender by the outside label because there was none. I opened it slowly contemplating what could be enclosed and from whom. I finally got the envelope opened all the way and took out the paper that was contained therein.

First my hands began to shake, my body became weak, and my mind froze. Then suddenly, an overwhelming feeling erupted straight from the pit of my stomach. I wanted to cry, could feel the tears building, but they would not come. I had to believe that the letter was just some prank of a jealous, selfish, loser who just wanted to hurt me.

"Why me dear Lord and why now? I'm about to get married and I love this man."

I pleaded desperately not knowing what I should really believe or even think. My mind was doing eighty-five on a regular road and if I did not stop I knew I was about to crash. I ignored the sound of my ringing phone as my dreadful fears clung to me like leaches. Somewhere in my mind I wanted to believe that what I had just read was going to be denied. However, just like before my mind knew better than what my heart wanted it to believe. My answering machine came on, but I only caught the beginning of Sheria's message before my mind totally became stone again desperately trying to float on water.

Soon after the machine clicked off I heard keys in the door and anticipated Chris's arrival. I wanted him to save us through denial. At any other time his melodious voice would have been a sexy turn-on for me, but that time my heart burned. He stood tall in the doorway, his neatly braided hair hung past his shoulders, eyes sparkled and teeth demonstrated glee.

"Hi baby! What's going on?" Chris asked.

He attempted to come closer, however, I disrupted his aim.

"Did you sleep with her?"

The keys fell from his hands, his eyes displayed worry, and his teeth concealed themselves. He stood still in his tracks.

"Uhm...What do you mean baby?"

"Don't try to insult my intelligence Chris! Please answer the question or were there more than one?" I bellowed.

"Uhm... ah...Celine... baby..."

"What's the matter Chris, can't find your fucking tongue?"

"I'm sorry baby..."

"About what Chris?" I shouted.

By this time I was furious and did not care if it showed.

"It was only once I swear. I tried to tell you but I did not know how, baby please forgive me."

"How could you Chris?" I cried.

That was my breaking point as I was unable to control my tears any longer. I blazed inside as the anger and hurt came out as a flowing river. My reddened, tear-stained face was not a sight to behold as my heat radiated about the room. I pulled a napkin from the dispenser on my center table and blew my nose.

"It was an accident Celine. I really did not mean for it to happen."

"Get out of my house! Leave my keys and get the hell out!" I barked.

I was furious to have been played for such a fool. And even more so because I allowed myself to fall in love with him.

"Celine, let's talk about this honey. Pleeaase!"

"Don't you honey me! I was about to marry you, marry a liar. And our whole marriage would have been meaningless."

"Forgive me, I love you!"

"Where was that thought while you were fucking her? Huh?"

"Cel..."

"Get out now Chris before things get any worse."

He turned around and started heading in the direction he had appeared from earlier.

"Leave my keys!"

He placed them down on a table in the center of the room on his way out. I could see Chris facing my direction from the corner of my eyes that refused to look at him.

"I do love you Celine, and I'm really sorry."

I heard the door close and then my tears came pouring down again like a heavy rainstorm.

My brain was shot and I needed someone to be there with me. Rob should have been the last person to cross my mind, but he was the one I opted and called anyway. I sat there after hanging up the phone, unable to think, cursing like a sailor in my mind. I loved Chris and I hated him. I did not try to stop the tears as they rolled uncontrollably.

I opened the door and he immediately took me into his comforting arms.

"I'm sorry. I didn't mean to bring my burden down on you, but I did not want to call anyone else."

"Don't worry about it babe, I'm glad you called me. You know I'm here for you."

Rob kissed my forehead and my body tingled all over.

"You don't have to talk about it if you don't want to. I'll just stay until you feel better."

I gestured toward the television absently.

"Movie?"

"Whatever you want," he replied.

I decided to try some happy medicine. I went into the kitchen and came back with a bottle of Remy Red. Rob sipped from the glass that I gave him. I filled mine to the very top and took a really big swig. I sat on the couch with Rob's arm around me while we watched a re-run of Everybody Loves Raymond. We laughed and when the happy medicine started kicking in my laughter became even more profuse. Within twenty minutes I found myself kissing on Rob and that's the last thing I remembered from that night.

In the morning I laid in my bed wearing a tee shirt and my panties. My vision was blurred, so I tried to orientate myself. My palm found the side of my head and tried to offer protection from the drum that was beating inside. Then bigger concerns crossed my mind.

"What happened last night?"

Chris

My new store officially opened today and I had music and snacks to welcome new clients, as well as to thank the old ones for their continued support. Luckily, for me I had such a good friend in Pete as he gladly accepted being my host for the day. Otherwise, I perhaps would have postponed my opening date in fear that I would not have made the best host at the time. In my line of business good customer service was everything.

"Yo man, this bookstore business is fly. So many customers already," Pete commented.

"Well, most of them. Some are regulars from my old spot who just came by to check out the new spot. Besides, it's all about location baby, and this side of Brooklyn is kicking."

"Shit seems tight son."

"Thanks. It's a good thing man, I really busted my butt getting here."

"I know that bro and I'm proud of you. Well, I better get back to hostin'."

Pete laughed slyly as he started to move away.

"Hey, no funny business," I warned.

I smirked at him knowing that he knew that business was business and pleasure did not ever get mixed in.

As Pete walked away I looked past him towards the entrance and saw a woman pass by. Her curvy hips printed nicely in faded blue jeans with a white tube top and sneakers. She wore her hair up in a bun and had on earrings that dangled towards her shoulder blades. I did not know how I spotted so much detail in such a short time, but that was irrelevant at the time. My instincts immediately told me to run after her, and I did.

"Celine?"

I grabbed the woman's arm. She flinched and turned around frightened out of her skin. Then I realized that the enlarged light green eyes did not belong to my baby.

"Sorry, thought you were someone else."

I barely muttered the words to her as I walked away. I hoped that she heard me, yet I did not really care. My mind was in chaos. I really had to get out of there and get some rest.

"Pete, my man can you handle things around here for me. Need to go home and rest a bit."

"That's cool man, You know I got your back. I'll call if I need anything."

"Thanks man."

"For sho'."

On my way home I dialed her number and was greeted by the recorded sound of her voice. I had called numerous times before and so I knew that Celine was purposely ignoring my calls. Because of that reason I decided against leaving a message. I got home in a devastated state of mind, and was punished even more when insomnia hit me and caused my eyes to become almost blood red. I had lost my appetite and felt very much disabled. Pain ate my insides and unstoppable tears flooded my heart. I hoped and wished that everything would go back to normal, still my desire remained out of bound.

Unexpectedly, my mind drifted to Brenda and the fact that she was the only person to have sent that letter. I was unsure of why the *why*, *how* or *who* did not occur to me before. But, at that very moment I wanted to find Brenda and make her wish that she had never met me

Sheria

I was in my cold apartment dressed in a bunch of clothes praying for the heat to come up soon. I had one of those 'cheap with the heat' Landlords and he was working my last nerve. He would put on the heat for a few minutes and just as the house began to warm up it would shut right back off. This made me feel like I would have preferred for it to have been off all the while instead of giving an occasional tease. I had promised myself to remain calm, but when I called Mr. John minutes before he had gotten nasty with me. Therefore, I was forced to threaten reporting him to the Department of Housing.

Just as I finished tinkling and got back in the room I heard that noisy sound announcing the boosting up of the heat. I laid back on the bed and tried to steal some of my comforter's warmth. I had stayed home that Saturday morning because my self esteem was at an all too familiar low. I was unsure of myself and so I sulked at home in drowning despair. I could not explain the emotions that bombarded my life every now and then. All I knew was that with each day it got worse. One minute I was fine, and the next I felt disgusted with myself. My mother constantly crossed my mind. Although she was in her own world out there somewhere, I knew exactly what she was up to. There were no doubts in my mind that she was strung out somewhere with one of her partners, if she was still alive anyway. In the times of my emotional sink I found myself in a struggle as I tried to persuade myself that I was nothing like her.

Eventually, I would become stuffed-up from crying too much. Sleep would then conquer me, then I would awake again, only that time to my usual self. I would pick up from there and go on about my life the way that it had been since my father left us, and she left me.

Celine

Having my whole body become numb did not help any to stop my tears from coming. I repeated to myself again and again that everything would be ok, that I would feel better soon, and that Chris was not worth my tears. And although, I knew that I should not have, I reread the letter about ten times. Each time, I tried to fool my eyes that they were disillusioned because I had read each of those heart breaking words incorrectly. However, my heart would be blundered all over again, and again, and again since the words became more deadly apparent.

It was Monday morning and I woke up to a tear-soaked pillow. As if crippled, my body muscles fought with me as I rolled over more to the left side of my bed to retrieve the phone. An unidentifiable dry hand stretched for my phone and picked it up while the other reached up and scratched my itchy, tear-stained face. I pressed the talk button, but found that my job number was registered nowhere in my head. I thought about the way I knew that number so well like the back of my hand, yet right then even the first digit was nowhere to be found in my memory bank. I reached for my pocketbook and searched through it with little life. When I came back up with nothing I scanned through the saved numbers in the cordless phone.

"Good morning A & J's Law Offices. Ellen speaking, how may I help you?"

"Hi Ellen this is Celine, I won't be coming in today."

"Everything ok?"

"Just not feeling too good."

"Hope you feel better soon."

"Thanks, bye."

I rolled back over on the bed after replacing the phone in its cradle. My body ached with every motion. My mind performed tiring overtime as I tried failingly to put out all of its negative contents. Finally, I dozed off, yet thoughtless pain would not allow me to sleep and so I awoke again within the next hour. My desperate struggle this time, to balance and get up instead of permitting the weight to pull me down, allowed me to succeed. My legs stumbled lazily one after the other and managed to get me to the bathroom in two minutes. I set the water temperature and began to undress regardless that I was barely able to even stand. When I stepped into the tub, the sudden hit of water combined with the steam revived me instantly, even though it did nothing to ease my hurt. Then suddenly the ringing phone stole my momentary peace. Unaware of why I felt a strong need to answer it, I stepped out and ran a trail of wetness into my bedroom, retrieved the phone, and hurried back into the bathroom.

"Hello?"

"Hi!"

"Hey Sher, what's up?"

"Is everything ok? I called your job and your secretary said you were out for the day."

"Yeah I'm ok. Just didn't feel like going in today. Just need a day off you know?"

"Are you sure?" she asked with much concern.

"Yeah."

"So what are you doing today then?"

The last thing I wanted at this point was to have Sheria worrying.

"I'll probably go downtown."

"I was wondering if you wanted to see the Madam Toussant Museum. I have four tickets."

"Maybe some other time sweetie."

I did not even have to think about it because I knew that being in there would only bring back memories of Chris and I.

"You sure?" Sheria asked.

"Yeah."

"I'll come by and see you later ok? Gotto go before this hawk land on my back."

"Don't let your supervisor hear you calling her that."

We both shared a laugh.

"Alright see you later."

"Bye."

I got up from the toilet seat and went back in the shower. I felt the tears emerging again.

"You need to be stronger than this Celine."

My inner voice scolded me, but I did not know whether it was enough.

Celine

Friday at work I could barely function. I had been second-guessing myself since I made my decision on what I would say to Rob.

"Hey Celine!"

I looked up and it was George, a Hispanic attorney whom I worked with.

"Oh hi George."

He was walking by my office, but had backed up and peeked his head inside the door.

"You alright?" he questioned.

"Yeah!"

I tried to sound convincing, but I doubt that I was able to do a good job.

"You sure? You don't look too good."

"I'm fine. Just something on my mind."

"Want to talk about it?"

"Nah," I replied with a funny face to assure him that I would be alright.

"Ok, if you change your mind you know where I'll be."

"Thanks George."

"Anytime."

George was a good man who took his work very seriously. He had been married for fifteen years when his wife, with whom he had two kids, "just upped and ran off with another man". He was devastated and since then had thrown himself even deeper into his work. His light-skinned, medium height, thick frame was harsh with his opponents in the courtroom. And that demeanor quickly helped to rank us as one of the best firms. My mind snapped back and once again I was left to contemplate thoughts in my head. I thought about what Sheria had said to me a week earlier. After serious deliberations, I decided that she really made sense. I had to take some cold medicine to de-clog my nose so I would be able to 'wake up and smell the coffee'. It did not take very long for me to reach my realization, and so I arranged to lunch with Rob.

We met at an Italian restaurant not too far from where we usually ate. My appetite was not too great so I intended to only have a regular salad with Italian dressing. When I arrived the time was twelve ten p.m. and Rob was already there. I went over and joined him at the corner table next to a huge window that provided lots of visibility of outdoors.

"Hi Rob," I greeted.

"What's going on?"

"Nothing much."

He greeted me with a hug and cheek kisses as usual. I sat opposite to him and picked up a small, thick menu that opened into two.

"What are you having?" I asked.

Chicken parmesan with some spaghetti," he replied.

"Sounds good. I'll try the same."

While we waited for the food to come I wanted to tell Rob and get it over with. But I knew better to wait until lunch was over so there would not be any uncomfortable moments between us. The waiter returned and we gobbled our food with little verbal contact. In less than no time we were finished eating.

Although I felt guilty about my next few words I knew they had to be said.

"Rob I asked you to lunch because I want to tell you something."

"Shoot," he said.

He was so easy going as he probably imagined some other words leaving my lips.

I looked out the window to my left. There were some birds on the not so busy side walks. My eyes followed a couple as they passed by hand in hand with smiles glued to their faces. Thoughts of Chris bombarded my mind. I really did not want to hurt Rob's feelings.

"What is it? Go ahead, am listening," he said.

I turned back my attention towards Rob.

"Well, I want to discontinue seeing you," I said.

I had re-run the situation in my mind a thousand times before that moment, and tried to figure out the best way in which to say what I had to say. But, I doubt there was any in existence so I decided to just hit the nail directly on its head without missing.

"You're a wonderful person, however, I can't see you anymore. I am not interested in you intimately and therefore do not want to mislead you in anyway. Also, I did not like the way things almost got out of control the other night."

"But nothing happened. And we're just friends," Rob protested.

"Regardless, I still believe this is the right thing to do," I assured him.

"You're a good part of my life Celine, a great friend," he pleaded.

My heart was broken by his words. I really had not meant for things to get so complicated between us.

"I'm sorry Rob, but it just has to be. I'm so sorry. You're a wonderful man."

"So why do I have to lose you?"

"Goodbye Rob."

I kissed his cheek, put down enough money to pay for both our meals plus tip, and walked away.

Chris

"This is the worst situation I ever had to face cuz. And to think that it was only a mistake makes it even worse because I am not the person to do this kind of shit."

"You're gonna have to get over it dude. I know what you're saying and how you feel but it's more difficult than you realize," Pete countered.

"I know. Can't really blame her for her reaction, but I wish there was a way for her to see how really sorry I am, and that I care for her a lot."

"If it's meant to be then it'll happen in due time. Don't worry 'bout it."

"Wish it was that easy."

Pete and I finished exercising and had decided to grub on a few slices of pizza in a local store before parting. My distress over Celine had really worn me down, which had ignited our particular conversation.

"Anyhow, enough about me. What's up with you and Sharon?"

I had to change the subject because it was bad enough that I spent my days moping over Celine. Being that I had Pete's company I just wanted to relax my mind to at least maintain what remained of my sanity.

"We aight. For the first time in a good while I'm enjoying chilling with someone."

"Sounds like things are getting serious between you two."

"Could be. We're getting along so far because she has such a easy going personality. There's no bickering yet, which is definitely a good thing because I'm passed that."

"For you to actually see one person for more than two weeks things must be good. Well, I'm happy for you man, just don't make the same mistake that I did."

We finished our pizza slices and each drank a medium cup of Pepsi soda.

When we got back to our cars we slapped hands in our own special way and pulled each other in.

"I'll talk to you later cuz," I said.

"Sure, peace."

Pete jumped in his red convertible and I jumped in my car then we pulled off in different directions.

I got home and immediately broke the promise I had made to myself. I know I shouldn't have but I had to hear her voice if only on her answering machine. I hardly even knew of a way to explain the way that I missed her. Since the day she entered my life, she played sweet music from my heart as though it was a violin.

"Hi this is Celine, please leave a message including your name and number and I'll get back to you, bye."

I hung up and renewed my ritual of late. I laid on my bed and moped.

Chris

My bookstore opening had gone very well, it was just unfortunate that I was not there. It was Friday evening and the weather was in the mid-sixties. I had already done my rounds of checking the bookstores for the day. Although I had two very dedicated managers I knew that it was not really good to be too trusting of anyone. Therefore, I checked my assets daily. I looked at my watch and noted that I had an hour before Celine would leave work. The waiting period for Celine to come around had become more than I could take, so I decided to take things into my own hands.

On my way I stopped at a Burger King drive through and ordered myself a chicken sandwich meal. My first thought had been to go by her job. But, afterwards I thought it best for me to just go by her house instead. I arrived and was still ahead of her by at least fifteen minutes so I parked my car out of sight and filled my growling belly. As soon as Celine pulled up I quickly revealed myself from my hiding spot. I ran up to her before she had a chance to get inside.

"We need to talk! You can't keep ignoring me," I said.

The house keys dropped from her frightened hands and she spun around with fury on her face. At the sight of me her eyebrows got ruffled, then she spun back around as if I was invisible. Celine retrieved her keys from the ground.

"Can I come in?" I asked.

"There's nothing for us to say to each other."

"I love you Celine."

Celine turned around with disgust in her eyes and her chest did a number underneath her shirt.

"You have no right to speak of such a word because you don't know what it means."

"I made a terrible mistake, and though I wish I could change it, I can't. Please give me a chance Celine, I need you in my life."

"You should have thought about that before you...you..."

Tears filled her eyes and she turned away to conceal her hurt. My heart bled knowing that I was the one that caused her pain. I moved closer behind her and put my right hand on her shoulder. She shrugged it off immediately.

"Don't you dare touch me with hands you put on another woman!" she snapped.

Her scream was frightening and I backed away to put a little distance between us.

"I'm sorry Celine. All I need is a little time to speak with you."

She finally got her door opened. She stepped inside, and with her back still turned towards me she spoke.

"We do need to talk Chris, but not right now. This has been difficult for me and it's even harder to understand. I'll call you so we could meet somewhere and speak."

Before I could even muster up a reply she closed the door. I stood there another few minutes mad at myself for bringing us to that point. But then I left happy that I got a chance to see her beautiful face. Celine was disappointed in me, still I had hope for us. So I went home thinking of ways that I could show her just how much I really loved her.

Celine

How much more could go wrong? Life just was not being fair to me lately. I really did not know what to expect next. I laid on my back on my queen-size bed and stared ahead at the blank, white ceiling. I looked there for answers to the many questions that flowed in my mind. Although deep inside I knew they would never come, I searched anyway. My phone rang again at eight p.m. I knew it was Chris, but I still looked at the caller's id. I so badly wanted to answer because my heart missed him more than anything, however, he hurt me. My hands and heart would not dare disobey my mind.

The answering machine came on and I heard the click as he hung up. Perhaps he was tired of leaving unanswered messages.

The ring on my finger looked a bit dim from soap residue. I studied it just lying around my finger as if it was made only for that purpose, to be there, on *my* finger. I thought about the tears that had streamed down my face when I said 'yes', and the smile that stayed on his when Chris asked me to marry him. I remembered loving him. I still loved him. But my heart was full of pride and things just were not that easy. I gently slid the ring from its comfort spot and tucked it far away out of my sight. Suddenly, I was in need of a vacation, so I decided to go visit my parents.

I do not know exactly when I fell asleep, but I awoke to the ringing phone again. I reached my hand over and lowered the ringer then drifted right back off again.

Chris

Something did not feel right. I had a nauseated emotion in the pit of my stomach. My body became hot and flushed, but I tried to shake the feeling off. I had left my first book store moments earlier and was on my way to the other to make sure that everything was in order. I was crossing the road to get to the opposite side where I had parked my car about a half an hour before. As I got to the middle of the street my heart began to thump against my chest even faster, my pupils dilated, my mouth opened in an O, and the scream that fought to come out stifled inside of me. I tried to move quickly enough but like glue held them, my feet stubbornly refused to move. The car screeched and the next thing I knew I flew in the air, then landed abruptly about two feet away from my original stance.

All around me I heard loud commotion of people from every direction stating what they had witnessed.

"Don't move, you can hurt yourself even more," a kind feminine voice offered.

Even if I wanted to I knew I could not. Moments later the ambulance arrived and the pain to get my body in all the right equipment was horrendous. I heard them say something about critical condition before the paramedics hurried me away to the nearest hospital. I was unable to catch the name, however, it seemed as though the police had caught the person who had hit me. What remained striking in my head though, was the fact that my accident was actually considered to have been intentional.

Celine

"A coma?" I asked.

"Yes, I'm afraid so."

There was a pause before the short, stubby, high yellow skinned doctor continued.

"He sustained multiple injuries including broken bones and his body went into instant shock."

"Will he be alright? How serious is it?" my quivering voice managed to expel.

"Right now we are unable to say, but be assured that we are doing the best we can. The rest depends on how long he stays in the coma; the longer he stays the more difficult his recovery will be. The fact that he did not fall into a coma right away is a good thing on his part though. As soon as we have anything new we will be sure to update you."

"Thanks doctor, may I see him now?"

"Sure."

He looked like such a peaceful baby asleep. Chris suffered a broken hand, a broken leg, and some other fractures. I touched the half of his index finger that was free and tears instantly fell from my eyes.

"I love you Chris, please don't leave me."

I had been in Florida when my cell phone rang and the horrible news was communicated to me. I immediately then booked my departure on the next outbound flight. On my arrival in New York I took a cab straight to LIU Hospital to be by his side. My mind ran all over the place and kept me devastated and flustered. Mad was overcame by sad when I realized that my fear for losing Chris was bigger than my anger. In that moment, I knew I loved and needed him more than anything in my life. Yet, one question flashed back and forth in my mind, *"can there be another chance for us?"*

Sheria

"Oh honey are you ok?" I asked.

I went over and hugged her tightly.

"I just got your message and came right away," I continued.

Celine's eyes were red and puffy and her skin so pale that if we had not known each other for years she would perhaps have been hard to recognize. I could not stand to see her so tortured, but I knew just how she felt. I could tell from the tear stains on her face that she had been crying not too long ago. She returned my hug and instantaneously started to bawl again.

"It's okay honey, he'll be fine."

After a good five minutes Celine finally released me and stood back like she was about to say something. She stopped in her steps and stared at the woman standing next to us.

"What the hell are you doing here?" she aggressively asked the woman.

In turn Brenda took a few steps backwards aware of the situation and not really wanting to cause any chaos.

"Um... Celine she came with me," I responded for her.

"You know this woman?" Celine blared.

"Yes, we met a while ago," I confessed.

"What the heck is going on here? Do you know that this is the woman that Chris slept with?"

"Yes, I know." I admitted.

"I'll just leave, I'm sorry for showing up here. I should have waited outside or something, don't know what I was thinking."

Brenda started to walk off.

"I'm sorry. I'll be right there Brenda, just wait for me."

I threw her my keys and she instinctively caught them and continued to walk away. I turned to Celine only to see a stronger depth of hurt on her face.

"I'm sorry about this, it's my fault. After I got your message I just rushed here not remembering that you two know each other."

Celine just stood there firm and stared ahead as if it was a ghost walking away from us and not actually a normal person.

"I don't believe you Sheria. And I can't even remember you telling me about your little meeting with Brenda."

She spoke with disgust and slight jealousy.

"What the heck is really going on here? You know what? As a matter of fact don't tell me. Just go and don't keep Brenda waiting for you."

As soon as she spoke the last word I was faced with Celine's back as she took large steps away from me.

"Celine! Please wait, there's something I need to tell you."

"I'm not interested, leave me alone!" she barked.

I obeyed her request and turned away to meet Brenda in my car.

"Sorry 'bout the confrontation just now. I was not thinking, should have told you where we were going," I said.

"What the heck is going on Sheria? Why didn't you tell me about Celine and Chris before? Is there something you're not telling me?" Brenda asked.

"Just did not want it to be a big deal. I've been friends with her forever and when you and I became acquainted I thought you were cool also. That's why I kept hanging out with you. I realized that even though you two could not get along with each other for your own reasons, I got along with each of you personally," I explained.

Brenda's expression became blank as she stared off into a land only she could see. Then after moments of silence her voice appeared again.

"How is he?"

"I don't really know," I responded, "think he's still in a coma."

"She really loves him, doesn't she?" Brenda asked.

"Yes. She does," I answered.

I could only imagine the regret that Brenda felt for having lost such a good man. But there was nothing to do. She knew it, and so did I.

"It's okay I'll catch a bus. You can go back inside because she needs you right now," Brenda said.

"No, I have to give her some time to calm down. She's going through too much right now and debating with me will only anger her even more. I'll call her later tonight."

"You sure?"

"Yeah, I'll call her later because she needs a breather. Besides, I have something to tell her that is no good news at all."

Chris

Her voice was as lovely as I could remember. She was so caring and always held my hand while she tried to assure me that everything would be fine. It sounded as though she was also trying to convince herself in the process of persuading me. Nevertheless, I gripped on to her words and tried harder to fight to break away from dreamy land back to the surface of reality.

"I love you Chris please don't leave me," she said.

I listened as Celine attempted to stifle her cries. I guess that she did not want me to sense her hurt and become scared. But it only made me stronger as I wanted to break free so I could hold her again. So I could be the strong one who reassured her that things would fall in place once more. I experienced her tender touch on my face and smelled her intoxicating, natural scents as she brought me down memory lane.

"Do you remember when we first met? Oh! The whole world around me stopped that night. You had effects on me I never imagined possible. I can recall the way that I stammered nervously because of how entirely taken I was with you. I don't think I ever told you this but I thought it directly when we met; you have such beautiful eyes. And yes I did get lost in them although I was not accustomed to chatting with strange men. There was something different about you, something magnetic."

Celine traced my lips before planting a soft, sensuous kiss on them.

"Even on our first date I wanted desperately to jump your bones. I went through great measures keeping myself under control. I knew you were the one because I had never felt for anyone the way I feel for you. And I know some people still consider 'love at first sight' to be silly, but baby I guess I was silly because I swear you had me hooked from the start."

There was a long pause while she contemplated her next set of words.

"I wish things had gone differently for us, but there probably is still time to make this work."

Her voice began to tremble. I could visualize her lips shaking and fresh tears forming in her eyes.

"I love you baby and I miss you. Please come back to me."

At that moment I wanted to just squeeze her to make us one, and inseparable. I wanted to make her mine forever and never look back. But, I helplessly could not. Then I heard her saying she'd see me later because Pete wanted to see me. I wanted to hear my boy's voice too, but I most desperately did not want Celine to leave. I vowed to myself that I would make things right; just how I was unsure because I was still stuck below reality.

Celine

I finally had to leave Chris for a while. I had just gotten home. I plopped down on my couch after dragging my suitcases just enough inside so I was able to close the front door. Boy was I ever drained because that one day had seemed like a day and a half to me. I could not even begin to focus on any one thing because so many thoughts crowded my brain. My feet went up after I laid back on the chair and I felt my body giving in to exhaustion. But, just as I felt that last piece of sweet relaxation taking over, the musical rhythm of my doorbell sounded through.

Frustrated, I looked at the clock that stood to the left in alignment with my body. It read eight p.m. and I wondered to myself who could be at my door. At first, I tried to ignore the call thinking that surely whoever it was would leave after a while, nevertheless, the person was relentless in their obvious mission to get my attention. I eased up slowly and glided across the room wishing without hope that the person would go away.

My brows instantly got wrinkled when I peeked through the peephole in the door.

"What on earth is he doing here?" I asked myself.

The question was rhetorical, as I did not really want to know. But I guess I was about to find out regardless being that he was so persistent. I opened the door and made no attempt to change my mood.

"Hey Celine, what's up?"

He grinned from ear to ear as though seeing me meant the world to him.

"Not feeling too well, what are you doing here?" I asked nonchalantly.

"Was in the neighborhood and just decided to stop by and see how you were doing."

"I don't mean to be rude, but I was asleep. Not feeling too good."

"Can I do anything to help?" he asked.

"No, I just need to go back and get some rest."

"Just let me come in a while to make sure everything's fine."

He was so forceful at times and I hated to hurt his feelings. Besides, I thought that the sooner I gave in the sooner I would have been left alone.

"Ok, just for a little while."

I opened the door enough for him to enter and locked it behind him. He strolled in and sat comfortably on the chair that I laid on only moments earlier. I went and sat on the chair opposite him.

"So how have you been Rob?" I asked trying to be polite.

"Been fine. Just wanted to see how you were doing. I know you said we should not see each other anymore, but we're still friends right?"

I could not even decipher why he would just show up at my home. And, the way my mind was operating overtime on other things I could not focus to even begin to think about what was taking place. My phone rang then, but before I could get up Rob was there turning down my ringer and messing with my answering machine.

"Don't answer it, you shouldn't be bothered right now," he said.

My body, suddenly with thoughts of it's own, trembled with fright. I tried nervously to not make it apparent, however, I was unable to. He came over and kneeled down by my chair.

"You okay babe? I'll take care of you."

"What's going on Rob?" I asked.

"Shhh!"

He placed his index finger gently over my lips to shut me up.

"Just relax, I'll give you a massage."

Rob then stood and went behind my chair. I felt his fingers dig deep into my shoulder blade muscles slowly making me high. My eyes rolled back in my head as I got into the mind blowing movements of his hands. He moved around until he was positioned in front of me.

"Lay on the floor so I can rub your back."

At first I hesitated. But then thought about all that had happened lately and decided I needed it. I moved in one motion from the chair to the comfort of my soft rug. Almost immediately I felt Rob's hand again, this time all over my back. My eyes closed in reflex and allowed all tension to leave my body. His fingers dug into my flesh, my rib cage, along my spine, the smallness of my waist. Then suddenly, I felt him pulling gently on my pants. I lifted my body just enough to allow my pants to be taken off then I relaxed again. I felt kisses on my neck that led down to my back. Something started growing on my ass, then I realized that it was Rob's pole. I turned around and he was naked like me, even more. He kissed my lips hungrily and I returned his gesture with just as much passion. The ringing of my bell brought me back to my senses, which caused me to push him away.

"Stop! Rob, stop it!" I shouted.

"They'll leave honey. Don't get it."

"No! This is a mistake, get off of me."

"You don't know what you're saying Celine. You want me just like I want you."

My bell continued to echo through like a siren, while I fought to get Rob off me.

"Rob please leave!" I begged.

By that time I was raging mad. I would have just hit him in the head with the nearest thing I could find.

"I love you Celine," Rob confessed.

He struggled to pull my legs asunder while trying to push his thick erected rod inside of me.

"No!" I screamed.

I pushed his chest and tried desperately to kick my feet up in an attempt to get him off. In spite of this, he overcame me when he pinned my arms above my head with one hand. With his knees parting my legs, his other hand guided the pathway. As the tip of his penis touched my precious vulva my front door flew open and Sheria stood there shocked. At the sight of her Rob quickly slipped himself inside me determined to accomplish his goal regardless. Sheria ran over and jumped on his back with her hands immediately taking residence around his throat. A second person ran inside and looked around in fury then she disappeared into an adjoining room. Finally, she came back with a frying pan and hit Rob upside his head. At that moment I recognized that it was Brenda as she ran towards Sheria who was gasped and cried from almost being strangled to death. I was in such trauma that I could hardly move.

"Call 911," I finally found back my voice to say.

Brenda picked up the phone and dialed the digits.

"911 emergency, how may I help you?" the person responded quickly and clearly.

"Someone has broken into the house and tried to rape her," Brenda reported in frantic.

"Where are you?"

"The address is..." she looked at me for direction.

"...between Linden and Hegeman," I chimed in.

Brenda repeated the address into the telephone.

"Is anyone hurt?" the operator asked.

"Yes, a woman is passed out from strangulation, and another raped."

"Is the intruder still there?"

"Yes. He is passed out also."

"Ok, hang tight the cops are on their way."

Brenda hung up the phone before the operator was able to tell her to stay on the line.

The wait for the cops to get there was one of the longest and hardest things for me. I sensed fear in Brenda's eyes also. Neither of us knew when or if Rob would regain consciousness before help came. We both knew that that would have been vile because I was still in a dire state, and Brenda looked weak and distraught. Brenda's dedication was apparent as she sat by Sheria's side the whole time and comforted her. Also, she kept watchful eyes on Rob for any unwanted movements. I also had my eyes planted on Rob like a hawk, even as I listened impatiently for any sound of an ambulance, police, or the fire fighters.

One of Rob's fingers jumped and I quickly grew frightened. My mind wondered with much impatience where the darn cops were. Then the same hand moved slowly towards his forehead then shifted back to his head where the frying pan had connected to him earlier.

"Urg!" he growled.

Brenda looked with wide eyes towards me and then towards Rob. Her quick reflexes allowed her to lunge for her previous weapon. But by that time Rob had jumped up and dived over to stop her. As they wrestled with the pan I got up, my body in aching pain, and walked over to them.

"Leave her alone Rob!" I shouted.

My attempt to distract him proved to be hopeless.

"Move back babe. I forgive you, don't worry because I know you didn't mean what you said before."

"You crazy son of a bitch!" I yelled.

I reached in the closet door in the living room and pulled back out.

"You'll be okay babe. You're just confused right now. You know I love you," he kept on.

"I know I'll be ok, but can't say the same for you. Now move back!"

That statement caught everyone's attention, I was the star of the moment.

"Dare me and I'll pump these bullets in you!"

I kept a gun being that I was a female and lived alone. And, although I never had a reason to use it before I was dead ass serious. I turned the barrel and pointed it directly between Rob's eyes. I had taken lessons so I knew enough.

"You won't do that. Honey, you know you love me just as I love you."

Rob spoke with a little less confidence than before, yet he didn't believe enough that I would really do it.

"Try me you crazy bastard. You have one second to move away."

Suddenly, cops came running in with guns drawn. One of them sensed that I was brainwashed to kill Rob and lunged in my direction to save both Rob and me. The cop got there just in time because although he did not get hit at the intended spot, Rob was hit. His body folded in half as he cupped his testicles in hand. Two other cops turned their attention to Rob. He bawled like a baby while one of the cops called for medical assistance for him.

"Are you ok?" the tall, dark skinned cop that had stopped me from killing Rob asked.

I shook my head, still in dismay.

Sheria was placed on a stretcher to be taken to the hospital. I waited in another ambulance to be carried away when Brenda walked up to me. Her left eye was swollen and discolored.

"I know this might not be the right time, but you need to know. Sheria wanted to let you know something at the hospital, which is what she came to tell you tonight. It is not my place to say so whenever you get a chance you should ask her."

At that moment all I could do was digest Brenda's information while I watched her walk away.

Sheria

When I opened my eyes, my head vibrated like a bell's toll, only louder. In automatic motion my hand flew up and rubbed the spot that jabbed the most. I heard the beep beep sound of machines, then saw the blurry figure of someone standing over me.

"Hey sweetie, you ok?"

I recognized the feminine voice and my lips instantly curled upwards while my eyes celebrated. My vision became clearer as she leaned down and kissed my forehead.

"Hey," I managed to utter.

Brenda leaned over and we gave each other a warm hug.

"Wait here so I can go get the doctor," she suggested.

I laughed to myself thinking that there was no way I could have gone anywhere even if I wanted to. She must have been so excited that I finally opened my eyes that she forgot. Within a minute Brenda came back accompanied by a sexy male doctor with luscious lips and a smile to die for.

"Hello Ms. Brookfield, I'm doctor Roy. How are you feeling?"

"I have a major headache. But aside from that I feel ok."

"I just need to ask you a few questions before I examine you thoroughly."

When the doctor finished recording details of the questions he asked me he took out his stethoscope and listened to my heart.

"Breath in and out," he commanded while pressing down the slightly cold instrument on my skin.

Dr. Roy stood still with his handsome self and paid close attention to his task at hand. Then he shined the light from a small object into my widened eyes, and inserted another into my ears and watched carefully.

"You look fine, but as procedure requires we have to run some blood tests just to make sure that everything is fine. I also recommend that you take a urine test. The nurse will be here in a few to assist you."

"Ok, thanks Doc," I said in a sexy flirtatious tone.

"You're welcome."

He smiled a seductive, 'knock my socks off' Denzel kinda smile before exiting the room.

"He said you should be leaving in a few, that's great!" Brenda walked back in and said.

"I know. Can't wait to get out of here," I replied.

"Celine's right down the hall so you should go and see her when you get discharged. I did not go to see her because I did not want to upset her."

"Is she ok?"

"Yeah, I told the doctor's I was her sister so they have been updating me on her state. She's fine; her parents are there with her."

"Yeah, I'll be sure to go see her when I get discharged."

As I sprawled there on the bed, confusion rushed back into my mind. I remembered what I still had to tell Celine. At any other time I would have been more than glad to deliver the purpose of the message. But under the circumstances I dreaded telling her what was really up.

Celine

My parents had just left to finally go and get some rest. They had been there the whole time for me and I wanted them to stop worrying so much. I knew that they had all the rights to worry because I was their only child and I really was not in a good state. However, I just wanted to protect them from having to see me in such bad shape. Although mom had insisted that she would return later that day, I did not feel too bad because at least I finally got her to go home for a little while.

I sat up and permitted my mind to stray towards Chris. I had called Pete earlier and he had told me that Chris was still in a coma. I was frantic about everything that happened within the past days and even more annoyed that I had no answers to the whys that constantly echoed in my head. Just as my life began to fall into place; just when I finally found real love and was about to seal it with recognized commitment; just when I was beyond happy for once, my world shattered right before my eyes. Worst of all nothing made sense in any way at all anymore.

"Knock! Knock!"

Someone seeking permission to enter my hospital room broke my concentration.

"Come in."

Sheria walked in and I saw an obvious sadness in her eyes.

"Hey sis! What's up?" I asked.

"Missed you girl," she replied.

She came over then and let her arms wrap themselves around me in the snuggest embrace. I returned the joy with a squeeze of my own.

"Missed you too. Are you ok?" I asked, concerned in more ways than one.

"Yeah, nothing major."

"How 'bout Brenda? Is she ok?" I asked.

"Yeah, she's outside in the car."

"And..."

"He's locked up."

There was a brief pause before Sheria continued.

"He sure is missing a screw. I can't imagine what his thoughts could have been why he did something like that."

"Still can't believe he was so evil, I trusted him."

"We all make mistakes Celine so don't torture yourself."

"So how are you feeling?" I asked.

"Much better. I had a massive headache that has gone so I can't complain. How's Chris? Have you heard anything?" Sheria asked.

"Still in a coma. I just hope everything goes okay and that he has a safe recovery very soon."

"He will, he's a strong man."

"I hope that's enough," I said distantly, "Everything was going so well untill... I really don't know what happened."

Tears formed in my eyes and I tried to blink them away.

"It's alright Celine, you'll get passed all this," Sheria comforted.

"Right now I can't see that far, but I really hope so," I sniffed.

Sheria wrapped her arms around me once more and this time I held on to her embrace as though it was our last.

"So you'll be checking out tomorrow?" Sheria asked.

"Yeah, the doctors need to evaluate me for another night."

"How are your parents?"

"Good, but I wish they didn't worry so much. They want to extend their stay for another week."

"Maybe it's good that they are here."

"I know they are only concerned, but I need space right now to deal with all that's happening."

"I understand."

Chris

I missed her voice. I was not sure of how long she had not visited me, but I was sure it was a very long time. *"Maybe she has given up on me,"* I thought in fright as I felt myself slowly drifting away.

I could not stop myself from thinking all the crazy thoughts that tortured my mind. I wondered whether Celine had loved me in the first place or maybe I had hurt her too much, and left her unable to face me even in such a painful state. At that moment the hate that I had for myself grew more because of what I had done to us. We had been so good together and I messed it all up big time.

Pete had come by earlier, but he had only stayed a short while. I figured that he did not know what to say in such a time. He was definitely my boy, had been since our eyes were at our knees. I could only imagine how devastated he felt as I would have felt if he was in a coma. He had touched my hand gently and said how much he loved and missed me. Pete had even encouraged me to hurry and get my behind back to reality. I remember how I felt like crying because I missed and loved him too, not to mention Celine. All that immobility and pent up feelings were tearing me apart. I only wanted Celine to come back and give me a reason to fight harder. I promised myself right then that if she came back and showed even the slightest chance of her still loving me, I would definitely overcome the demons that tried so hard to do me in.

I remembered the first time that we made love. It was so sensual and unique unlike anything I had ever experienced. The way that Celine had taken time out to organize the rose petals, the scented candles, and to cook dinner was so special. To top it off Celine had the splendid idea to place mistletoe above the bedroom door entrance. It was as clear as day in my mind; her soft peach looking skin against my toffee tone. I could still feel her warm, minty, breath arousing my facial nerves as it glided all over my body. Yeah, I missed her and that gave me reason to fight. Yet, it was not enough as my spirits wafted further.

Celine

Sheria wanted to be there also but I had rejected. My parents were already at the hospital to escort me home so I hardly saw the reason for her to be there too. Just as I had gotten home though, she called me as promised to make sure I was doing fine. My parents had hung a "Welcome Home Celine" banner on the walls and my heart melted as soon as I opened the door.

"Oh thanks mom and dad, you shouldn't have."

I smiled from ear to ear eating up all the attention of the only child that I was.

"We love you Celine and couldn't even imagine what would become of our world without you," mom said.

Tears came to my eyes because I knew they meant every word.

"Ahhhh, I love you guys too and I most definitely feel the same way."

I went over, hugged and kissed both of them. We all settled in to a well cooked meal of baked turkey, Spanish rice, plantains, steamed vegetables and a pineapple upside down cake courtesy of my mom.

"Mom the food is delicious," I recognized licking my fingers.

"Ain't it always child?" she boasted with a smile.

We all laughed knowing that she was far from lying.

I finally got through to my parents that I was okay and it was alright for them to go home. It was two days later, a nice mid- January weather when I took them to the airport. On my way home I made a few stops and was glad when I finally got home again. I went inside, kicked off my clothes and remained only in my bra and panties. My intention was to seriously meditate on what was happening in my life. As I sat on my bed I really did not know where to start. Looking around my room as though I was a visitor in someone else's place for the first time, I spotted a picture of Chris and I, taken a few months back. We were at the Woodbridge Mall in New Jersey and decided to get a disposable camera to take pictures. We took silly photos of each other until Chris suggested that we take one together. We looked around until I saw the kind face of an older looking man whom I had asked and he gladly obliged. During the pose, Chris, with his face next to mine had whispered "I love you beautiful".

God knew at that moment as I stared at the picture of us I could not help but think that I loved him too. However, I was unsure of how to forgive him or whether I could trust him again. He was the most charming guy that I had ever met and eighteen months was a lot to let go of. We needed to talk, that much I knew, but him being in a coma delayed and possibly changed a lot of things for us. The phone rang breaking my concentration.

"Hello?"
"Hi sweetheart!"
"Hey mom, what's up?"
"Your dad and I just got in."
"Oh, how was your flight?"

"Good. In fact your dad and I decided to go to Hawaii for a week."

"Really? How did that come about?"

"Yeah, it's been a while since we went on a vacation together."

"Well, I hope you guys have fun."

"You know we most certainly will."

"Where's dad?"

"Outside tackling a ball with his golf stick."

"Still acting like he's Tiger Woods, huh?"

We both laughed at that one. My father swore up and down that he could play golf, but we all knew better. His balls almost never went anywhere near his aiming hole, and that was only when he managed to hit them from starting point.

I had not told my mom about what really happened between Chris and I. She was so confident in our relationship and that scared me. But, she had said one thing to me that stayed in my mind. I recalled her exact words.

"Commitment requires love, strength and struggle through tough times. Things aren't always easy, but after you pass your obstacles they become trivial and you develop a stronger bond."

"Are you there?" mom asked.

"Yeah, I'm here mom."

"Alright then, I love you. And take care of yourself."

"Love you too mom. Tell dad hi for me."

"Ok will do."

"Bye."

Chris

When I heard her voice my heart rate instantly sped up. Celine finally had come to visit me again. Her smell filled my lungs and seemed as though it was the oxygen in the air that I needed to breathe. At first she was barely audible, but then I melted when I felt her small, soft hand in mine. Her fingers glided in silhouette motion as they caressed my palm. Next her fingertips touched my face, rubbed my cheeks, and danced over my eyebrows. I felt her strong energy and knew that she still felt deeply for me. Words could not even begin to explain how that made me feel, and so I summoned my body to move in beat with my mind. I wanted to get up, to speak with her. I wanted to tell Celine with more than words just how much she meant to me.

"Oh, Chris why did things have to go this way between us? I thought everything was fine, thought this was it - you were the one for me... until I found out about Brenda. Crushed is a tiny magnitude of a word to explain how I felt that day... and still feel now because something so wonderful was ruined."

"Stop it Celine. I love you baby. Saying sorry can hardly begin to explain how much of an asshole I feel like. I found it all with you and stupidly allowed one night to bring us so much misery."

"I know now that it was only one night. But it brought such heightened results that the one before the night does not really count. It might as well had been two, three, one hundred. There just wouldn't have been a difference."

"That was the biggest mistake of my life..."

"It might have been just a mistake but it's still hard to accept. I've been going through a lot lately and I just wanted to let you know, if you can hear me at all, that I probably won't be coming around here for a while."

"Why my sweet? Please don't do this. Celine, you're the beat in my heart, without you I have no life."

"Goodbye Chris."

Celine's lips electrified me with brief satisfaction over my entire body. Then as soon as the moment passed, tears poured like a heavy rain inside my heart. Celine spoke no more words. I thought right then that life, as I knew it, was over for me. My only battle remained with my unconscious soul, which was successful at keeping me from running after my baby. I don't know what exactly was going on in her head, but I wanted to wake up and take away all that did not belong there. I wanted to revive her, to revive us, yet I was too late. As I laid down my mind ran from me and my body faded deeper below the surface of reality almost reaching non-existence.

Sheria

I took tiny unwilling steps up to the desk and questioned the two-colored face woman after she got off the phone.

"Is doctor Peterson in?"

"Do you have an appointment?" she asked in a serious business tone.

"No, but I would like..."

"I can give you an appointment to come back because his schedule is full today."

"As I was saying this is an emergency and I would like to see him today," I stated hoping she would not give me further reason to black out on her.

Although I did not really want to know what was wrong I had to and the wait had been long enough.

"What's the emergency?"

"I had an appointment to come in a few days ago to discuss some test results he had called me about. However, I was in an accident. Therefore I was unable to make it."

The woman's face grew wrinkled like she was trying to decipher whether to accept my story or not. Then, after a few uncalled for silent seconds, she spoke again.

"His schedule is very tight today, however, I will check with him to see if we can fit you in."

"I'll be grateful," I replied half-hearted.

"Give me one minute, but it's no guarantee like I said," she insisted.

Ms Freckles repeated herself as if she had already concluded that I would not see Dr. Peterson, yet she would make me feel good about her at least checking.

My phony smile shined, "I'll wait over there."

My feet led me miserably to the waiting area that had nicely decorated upholsters elegantly placed in an artistic way. My discomfort shined as I sat among a room concentrated with mostly middle-aged women and about two men. General Hospital played on the television, which was mounted into a wall stand.

"Ms. Roberts?"

"Yes?" I answered the woman that I spoke to moments before, and walked up to her.

"He says he'll see you, however, there will be a wait because he has to take care of some of his patients that were here first."

"How long will the wait be?" I asked.

"I'm not sure, perhaps an hour or so."

"Ok thanks."

While I did not want to wait such a long time I knew I had no choice. I went back and sat in the same seat I had before. My eyes gazed around with my mind anxious just wanting to get the whole ordeal over with already. The nervousness that held me still threatened to worsen, as I sat not knowing what to think or do. Eventually, the boisterous pumping of my heart against my chest convinced me to go outside for a bit of fresh air.

As soon as I exited the glass doors of the building I was jailed into the unhealthy habits of two smokers. They each inhaled deeply as though they were taking their last breaths allowing the tobacco to properly poison their lungs before they exhaled. One of them, the gray haired bearded old man, puffed on his cigarette almost reaching half in just one pull. I quickly broke free and turned the corner for a fresher bulk of air. But the wild wind hit me head on and almost knocked me to the floor. I thought that the weather surely had changed in the few minutes that I had been inside. After a minute I went back inside because the wind chill felt like zero in Alaska.

Celine

"Good morning Ellen."
"Good morning, how are you today?"
"Marvelous and you?"
Ellen raised her eyes at my new, jubilant attitude. From the glee that danced in them I could tell my energy was rubbing off.
"Would you like to join me for lunch today, Ellen?" I asked.
"I sure would!" she responded.
"Well, lunch it will be. Is twelve good?"
"Yeah."
"Ok we'll decide then on where to eat. I'll be in my office."
After I called out on Friday and spent the weekend sulking about how cruel life was treating me, I wised up. I did not want to keep feeling pity for myself, and sure did not want to pass on the negative energy to everyone that surrounded me. So late Sunday evening I grabbed my purse and went to Express to snag me a new suit. With that I realized had to come a new attitude, which I was transformed with when I slid into my above the knee length black wool skirt suit. Ever since Chris entered my life I had focused on him as the center. After serious meditation and scolding myself yesterday I decided to go with the contrary and start to focus on myself. I had to find myself, and that meant that I had to leave all the sulking behind.

I stepped into my office and was overcome with more joy as the light shined through my large glass window, and fed me a bright and colorful surrounding. My warm, plush chair welcomed my buttocks providing the comfort of its soft material. My legs, with a mind of their own, lifted automatically and rested themselves on my desk top. Then my manicured fingers interlocked at the back of my head to provide support as I got comfortable. My lungs sucked up much air, then exhaled slowly.

"This feels good!" I stated with glee to the thin air.

After about five minutes I began going through my cases that had stocked up over the weekend. I grabbed the file at the top of the pile and opened the cream jacket.

"Darn it! Another sex abuse case."

It was just so bothersome how many kids were out there getting abused, especially by close family members and friends of the family. The saddest part was that, with people being caught up with responsibilities of trying to make ends meet, that kind of behavior usually went unnoticed for long periods of time. By then, the child is already affected in very deep and disturbing emotional, physical, and psychological ways.

My job was a very tough one because I had to defend cases that sometimes were so tumultuous, yet I had to refrain from getting emotionally involved. I had to learn to detach myself and accept that no matter how cruel a situation may seem that it was just a part of life. I could not act on my urge to ring a man's neck after he has killed his own wife and child because of a senseless jealous rage. Nor could I feel like I wanted to jail a woman for life because she has placed her child in a plastic bag, and suffocated it right after birth. But, what I do have to become is emotionless; I have to think as though I do not have a self. I have to force myself to realize that it is never about me no matter how I might feel. I quickly put aside my thoughts and delved into the case at hand. Within no time it was twelve p.m. and Ellen knocked on my door ready to go.

"Hey!" I said as she walked in.

"Ready? I'm starved," she replied.

Ellen had started working for me a couple months back after my other assistant also by the name of Ellen resigned and moved away for a promotion in another State. I had been so caught up with my own life affairs that I did not have time to get to know her better. She probably had settled in to thinking that I was such an antisocial person to work with.

"So where do you usually eat?" I asked.

"I normally bring my lunch from home, but last night I had been too busy helping the kids with their home work. By the time I got around to cooking it was too late."

"How many kids do you have?"

"Two, a boy and a girl."

"How old are they?"

"My son is twelve and my daughter two."

"Wow! You just had a baby? You look so in shape I can hardly tell."

"Thanks, it was not hard. Actually, contrary to what many people think after a few weeks the body bounces back into shape especially if you eat healthy throughout your pregnancy and afterwards."

There was a short pause while I held the door open for her as we exited the building.

"Do you have kids?" she asked.

"Nah, but hopefully some day I will."

"Heard you're suppose to get married soon, congratulations!"

I could feel the redness that captured my face after her remark. I was deeply embarrassed.

"It's off, long story."

"Sorry, I didn't mean to pry. I know what it must feel like because I've been down the divorce road and it wasn't easy. If you ever need to talk I'm always here."

"Thanks Ellen."

"Anytime."

My purge was all about strengthening myself so I knew I had to change the subject before I backslided.

"So where are you from originally Ellen," I asked.

"New Jersey, how 'bout you?"

"I was born here and I doubt I could ever leave. I think that once a person gets used to the fast life of the City nowhere else will do."

"That's so true because I came over here to attend school and after a few months I could not see myself going back. New Jersey is such a quieter lifestyle. I've settled in over here now."

I took her to the Spanish restaurant not too far down the street from our job where Rob and I often ate. The thought of him gave me a sudden shudder, however, I refused to let him instill fear in me. I was determined to move on with my life, which meant going about life my usual way.

"You could try the baked chicken with rice and beans, and plantains," I suggested.

"You had that before?" she asked.

"Yeah, the chicken is usually very tender and juicy on the inside with a nice golden color on the outside."

We chattered and got to know each other some more while we awaited our orders.

I had turned a new page in my life. Still, uncertainty would not leave me alone.

Sheria

I do not know how I functioned after that life-changing minute with Dr. Peterson. That light skinned, twisted face man opened my eyes and forced me to hear the words he spoke. His words still rang through in my mind days later as I sat home for the third straight day from work. I cannot believe that I had been so lax with my health.

"Knock! Knock! Sher?"

Celine's voice penetrated through my door and I wondered what she was doing there in the middle of the workday. I hardly felt the need for company, but I could not allow my best friend to stand outside. I knew that Celine was in a very concerned state so I willed myself to get up. My legs paced over to the door. My arms stretched lazily to open the lock and let her in.

"How you feeling girl?"

She walked in and without warning threw her arms around me in an attempt to comfort me. I responded in the same fashion and accepted her squeeze.

"I'm good. How 'bout you and what are you doing here?" I asked.

"Had to come and check on you. Called your job and they said you were out, but you did not pick up your house phone when I called."

"Oh, I'm sorry. I had turned the ringer off because I just needed some time to think."

"You ok?" Celine asked again.

"Yeah," I replied unsure.

"I know that you're worried Sher, however, you have to move on with your life. You have to be strong so we can fight this together. After all, the doctor said there might still be a positive chance."

"Can't believe I was so careless. I did not think about things that I would want in my future. If I had called for my results then they would have diagnosed me earlier."

"You can't be sure Sher. I know that we have to be strong about keeping up on test results from our doctors, but sometimes they forget or even overlook things."

"I know. I definitely will be more careful now, but I just hope that I will be able to have kids one day after all this. I know I have been careless, but I think I will want a family of my own one day."

"Let's not jump to any conclusion since you are still waiting for more results. Try to stir your mind in a different direction," she recommended.

"It's hard Celine."

Tears filled my eyes against my will. She hugged me again, and that time the tears came down.

"Let's go for a walk, you need some fresh air."

"Don't you have to get back to work?" I asked.

"Nah, I'll take the rest of the day off."

"No, no I'll be fine. You should go back because you were out a couple days just last week."

"It's not a big deal, I'll work late tomorrow to make up for today."

"Ok, thanks sis."

I gave in because I knew that her persistence would still not be overruled in the end. I knew that I needed her there for me anyway.

"That's what I'm here for Sher. Besides, you would have done the same for me."

"Let me take an Indian first," I said.

"Ha...ha...ha," Celine laughed, "you like taking Indians huh? Do you ever take a real bath?"

I made a sarcastic smiley face at her.

"Funny!" I stated.

"You know you my girl even if you don't ever bathe," Celine joked further.

"If you don't stop yo' shit I'm gonna have to bring your behind back to your good old country bumpkin ways."

"Uh, uh, oh no you didn't go there. I know my Aunt Fry was a bit countrified, but what that gotta do with me?" she tried to fake the funk.

"Remember you liked her accent so much that you wanted to be like her?" I asked.

Celine busted out laughing because she knew that I was not even lying. Looking back then I could not imagine what kind of plague had gotten over Celine for her to have admired her aunt so much. Her Aunt Fry is eight years older than Aunt Joy, Celine's mom. She was raised in California with her grandparents because her mother, Frida had conceived her at a young age. Frida had left Fry there and gone on a journey to 'make something of herself' and then go back for her. But when Frida went back for her, Aunt Fry did not want to leave, so she stayed with her grandparents. She visited her sister, Aunt Joy on a regular basis, especially since she had no kids of her own. As a child growing up, Celine had been very admirable of her.

"Her clothes used to always be so tight showing every curve of her body," Celine remembered.

"Yeah, and do you recall how much you liked that orange and green suit of hers that she wore with those special blue heels everywhere?" I wondered out loud.

"Ah come on, that's not fair. You've cracked on me enough. Time for you to go in the shower," she said.

"My Aunt Fry is sexy."

I imitated the words Celine once spoke only to regret it. My face was red as I doubled over in laughter.

"Hah! Hah!" she teased while making a funny face.

"Well, I must admit she had serious color blindness or perhaps she just lacked matching skills. But you have to admit that she was very shapely with that round behind of hers," Celine tried to put in something positive.

I continued to laugh and was joyful because Celine had helped to shift my mind from the stressful state I had been in only moments before. I finally calmed down and got up off the floor beside the couch where I had fallen.

"Ok she did have a 'I wanna tap that ass' behind. But girl had a extra serious problem getting the right match," I said.

"I love you Sher," Celine said.

"Where did that come from?" I asked.

"Just wanted to remind you."

"Love you too Celine."

"Alright girl stop tripping and get yo' ass in the shower."

"Ok, ok, I'm going."

Celine

Chris! The *one* thing that was crazy-glued to my mind. No matter how much I tried to stop them, thoughts of him penetrated my whole being and made me feel so lost. A part of me was missing and I was unsure of how much longer I would be able to continue that way. I started to spend long nights at my office with eyes, hands, and mind buried alive in stacks of cases. Whenever I was home, I drowned myself in the art of yoga. Still, void, emptiness, and loneliness would always find me. This was especially true at vulnerable times when I laid in bed trying to fall asleep. I never knew sleeplessness before, but insomnia had become my best friend.

I thought that I had finally been able to rid myself of the misery that blanketed me. But, eventually the temperance of my revival slapped me. To deal with my fears I chose denial, but like a wayward child reality chose me instead.

"Buzz! Buzz!"

I walked to the door and looked through the hole to see who was requesting my attention. He stood on the opposite side of my door with worried eyes and skin looking pale. My heart immediately began fighting with my chest, throwing hard punches mixed with fear. My hands trembled while my mind ran in various directions.

"Buzz!"

I jumped at the sound of the bell ringing once more. My mind tried to concentrate on getting me together before I opened the door, but the unknown had me very jittery. Slowly, I cracked the door open.

"Hi Pete, how are you?"

"Can I come in?" he inquired.

He was bold and to the point, even sounded a bit mad. I hesitated not really wanting to oblige him. Then after reconsideration I allowed him his request. Pete walked straight across my clean white carpet and sat in my living room as though he had been there before. I closed the door and went over to sit in the couch opposite him. He stood defensively then got to his mission at hand.

"When was the last time you went to visit Chris?" he barked.

The tone of his voice startled me as my eyes bulged in disbelief.

"What?" I asked with wrinkled lines across my forehead.

"He cared for you and this is how you treat him? By betraying him when he's on his death bed?" he accused.

"First of all, how dare you come in my house and scream at me. And secondly, I did not betray him, *he* was the one who betrayed me by going astray, so clear your memory and get it straight," I told him with much attitude.

"Get over it! You know, I was not surprised when Chris told me about his proposal to you because I saw that he was really digging you..."

"Get out of my house!" I yelled.

I pointed in the direction of my door.

"...I know that he hurt you, but although they were his actions they cut to the heart of his soul. He was so devastated and didn't even know what to do. Now he lays up in a hospital, in a coma, and all you can think about is yourself. Well, I say get the hell over it already! He loves you and if you have feelings for him that's all that should matter. You can either chose to leave him there to die by himself or to be there for him, which is what marriage is all about. And remember that you were the one that answered yes that you'd marry him."

I stood dumbfounded with a blank stare. Pete shook his head and walked towards my door then stopped with his back still turned towards me.

"Get the hell over it, he loved you. Would bet my life that he still loves you."

I could hardly tell that he was the same person that screamed at me only seconds before because this time Pete had a soft spoken, heart crushed, baby voice. He walked out and closed the door behind him. I sat back in the chair, mouth open, and body motionless. I could not figure out the nerve of that man to come in my house and act like that.

"But am I really being selfish?" I asked the air.

It was a question my brain was left to tackle.

Sheria

He walked in and sat at the bar about ten minutes after I arrived. From a distance he did not look like a 'pretty boy,' yet he was fairly attractive with a straight face. It was the suaveness of his walk and his bowed legs that first caught my eyes. He captured my mind and briefly made himself the focal point of my thoughts. A sudden shudder came over me and I knew I had to meet him. The shaking of my hands along with my heart fluttering like a bird in the sky made me wonder why this man had such effect on me. I foolishly debated back and forth with myself about getting up the nerve to invite myself over. Five minutes passed, then ten, and finally I stood, adjusted my ankle length jeans skirt and turtleneck short-sleeved sweater and strolled on over.

"Hi, my name is Sheria," I stated with an outstretched palm.

The man hesitated for about two seconds and that caused my heart to pound faster inside my chest as my emotions reddened from embarrassment. Just in time though, his sexy baritone exited his thin lips and excited me once more.

"Ricky, nice to meet you," he replied.

He took my palm into the softness of his own.

"Mind if I sit beside you?" I asked.

"No, not at all. Actually, I must say I'm impressed that a fine specie of a woman like you came over to chat."

"Women too could initiate friendship, no?" I asked.

"Absolutely, but I just don't see it often. I must mention that it is very refreshing because it takes some weight off the men," he pointed out.

I had been drinking a glass of Daiquiri Sour and brought it over with me. I took a sip of the small amount that was left and rested the glass back on the bar counter.

"I feel ya," I said letting him know I agreed with his thoughts.

"May I get you something else to drink?" Ricky asked never once taking his eyes off me.

"No thanks, I usually try to stick to one drink, especially when I'm out alone."

"So, you from around here Sheria?" Ricky asked.

"Yeah, I live out in Park Slope."

"Really, what side?" he asked more attentively.

"Close to the Botanical Gardens."

"Get outta here! I live not too far from there."

"That's just a couple blocks down from where I live. They have some nice houses over that side. I like to admire them especially during the Christmas time when most of them are all lit up with fancy decorations."

"Yeah, they be whiling with good spirits over there," he stated.

By the end of the night I was already captivated by how knowledgeable and mature Ricky seemed for his meager age of twenty-five.

"So, can I call you up some time?" he asked with widened eyes.

"Sure."

I put on my coat and then swung my pocket book over my shoulder. He stood and stared at me. All I could imagine was that I wish that I had met him at a more opportune time.

"Will I get your number to make that call possible?" he asked smiling broadly.

"Oh yeah, sorry. Ah…" I laughed, "I forgot my own number for a second there can you believe that? It's 555-558-5505."

"Wow! That's an awful lot of fives."

Ricky paused to tuck back his cell phone in his jacket pocket after saving my number.

"Did you drive?" he asked.

"Yeah," I responded.

"Ok, let me walk you to your car."

"Thanks."

"My pleasure."

By the time I got home I was seriously wishing that I had not met Ricky at such a tedious time in my life. My mind stirred wondering why we met at this time when there was no chance of us getting to know each other or even developing anything intimate. Just then my telephone rang and I marched over to get it.

"Hello?"

"Hey girl! Where you been? I've been calling you all evening."

"Went out for a drink after work."

"With who?" Celine queried.

"Myself. Just needed some time alone."

"So you just got in?" she questioned further.

"Yeah, what's up?"

I was not really in the mood to talk to anyone although Celine was my girl and all. I was not in the mood to be mothered.

"Nothing! I was just calling to see what was up with you," she said with concern in her voice.

My mind contemplated whether I should go ahead and tell her that I met a guy. But then I decided against it because I did not want her to take things the wrong way at all.

"Just here," I responded, "wanna go see a movie tomorrow?"

"Sure, straight after work or late evening?" she asked.

"Whichever you prefer. Tomorrow's Friday," I reminded.

"Alright."

"Call me tomorrow," I told her.

"Ok, I will. Bye."

Celine

The second day of February brought flurries with a forty-five degrees temperature outside. I stepped out decked in a pair of black fitted boot-cut jeans, a lime green turtleneck sweater and my black short Shearling opened up. My pointed Shearling trim heeled booties clinked on the ground with each step I took. I was doing my best to make myself feel good inside, still it proved to be a very difficult fight. Ever since Pete paid me his little visit earlier I had been feeling shitty about leaving Chris in the hospital alone. Yes, it was true that I felt deeply betrayed by his actions, but he was in a life and death situation. I needed to put my feelings aside for then.

"Hey lady! Why the pouting?"

I had gone downtown and stopped by the park close by my house on my way back home. Sheria had called looking for me and so I told her to meet me there. She got there in a little time since it was not too far from where she lived. My deep thoughts held me captive and did not allow me to notice when she walked up.

"Hey girl, 'sup?" I said.

I stood and gave her a tight embrace with our usual cheek kiss. I sat again this time she joined me.

"Been here long?" she queried.

Her nose was as red as Rudolph's, something that usually happened to her even when it was not much cold outside.

"No, about five or ten minutes," I answered.

"Looking sexy. Still, your mood doesn't quite go with the outfit."

"Got some things on my mind, that's all."

"Chris?" she figured.

"Yeah."

I told her about my altercation with Pete, or rather Pete's altercation with me. I had been hesitant about telling her because I knew she was going through a difficult time. I proceeded regardless because I really needed a sounding board before I went crazy with my bottled up thoughts.

"Can you believe he had the nerve to tell me off like that?" I questioned still in disbelief.

"He was wrong for confronting you the way he did, but..."

Sheria went silent perhaps trying to decipher whether she should continue.

"But what," I finally asked.

"Someone had to do it Celine."

"What do you mean by that?" I asked.

"You have to try and put Chris' betrayal behind you, life goes on. And don't bypass the fact that you're not so innocent yourself. We're all humans and we all make mistakes. He loved you regardless of his mistake and he needs you right now more than ever. You need to think about the fact that you were once willing to marry him because you loved him that much, and surely the love couldn't have just disappeared. Even if you can't be there as his woman, you should at least be there as his friend. He's in a very serious state and he needs you, he needs you."

I stood there and listened to the words I already knew but, had been too stubborn to admit to myself before. Tears glossed my eyes as I finally allowed the truth to permeate me. I was scared. But at that moment I realized that I could not allow fear to hold and comfort me anymore. I had to shake the denial that filled me.

"I do love him," I said eventually, "just don't know how to be either right now."

"Try."

Sheria suggested that so easily and it did sound simple for a hot minute. Yet I knew that it would take a whole lot more.

"I will, I'll try," I concluded.

"I heard from the doctors today," Sheria stated distantly.

"Is everything ok? What did they say?"

"I have to go in again to be rechecked," she replied.

Guilt rushed through me as I contemplated both our situations. There I was still hung up on the past, willing to allow the man that I loved to die without at least having my love and comfort. On the other hand there was Sheria dealing with a serious, perhaps life-threatening disease.

"What happened to the tests they just did?" I asked.

"The doctor needs me to do other tests to be sure of what he's dealing with."

"When do you have to go?"

"Next available appointment."

After a few more minutes of talking the winds began to kick up and so the park bench was no longer an appropriate place to be. I told Sheria I would call her later that day and we parted.

Chris

My sight was blurred and a massive headache pelted my forehead. Busy sounds of overworked machines and a few other unclear sounds captured my sense of hearing. My eyes squinted and widened involuntarily trying to adjust to the reflection of the light hitting my retinas. A few moments after my obscured eyesight cleared, my brain was able to declare that I was not home. My body felt robotic as my head slowly moved form side to side. My eyeballs darted around picking up details of objects in my environment to register to my brain for better comprehension of my situation. Finally, I deciphered that I was in a hospital or some kind of medical environment. I strained myself and brought life to my numbed hand in order to be able to press the call button that had been placed and clipped in my reach. Within seconds a middle-aged woman in a white lab coat rushed through the door.

"Welcome back Mr. De-Angelo!"

She smiled happily to see me as though I was her son.

"How do you feel? Do you remember what happened to you?" she bombarded me with questions.

"Feel like shit! Massive headache," I announced.

I lifted my now livened hand and rubbed my forehead to stress the location that hurt most.

"Do you remember your name?" she continued.

"Yes, Chris De-Angelo."

"How old are you?"

"Twenty-six years old."

Her smile broadened then to the point of showing neat, half-white teeth.

"How long have I been here?" I wanted to know.

"Four weeks. Do you remember what happened to you?"

"I think...I think I got hit by a car."

"Yes, you did," the hazel eyed Hispanic woman confirmed.

"Can I have something for my headache please?"

"Give me a second so I can examine you. Then I will give you some medication and call up your family."

The sound of the word family brought a smile to my face because Celine immediately came to mind. I missed her, but then my mind forced feelings on me that I did not understand. Intrusive thoughts that I did not want to hear or believe filled me.

"Ok, you look good so far. Temperature seems to be fine, I'll call up your family and then your doctor should be in to see you soon."

"Thanks."

"You're welcome."

I shifted the head of the bed upward so that I could sit at about a one hundred degrees angle. It was difficult moving my left arm due to it being strapped with needles that sent a variety of fluids into my body. Nevertheless, it cooperated some so I was able to move my hand a little. I shifted my body towards the left side towards the window and as soon as I settled again unwanted thoughts rushed into my head. Once again my thoughts were jolted, however, this time by the feel of someone's presence behind me.

"Is someone there?" I inquired.

I tried to turn back around and that was not such an easy thing to do. Silence rung through and so I did not ask again. I struggled until I was lying on my back once more. The sight of her caused me to freeze in my position. I was happy, sad, glad, and mad all in one. The tiring look on her face told me that her mind was working overtime also. Our eyes met head-on as we remained voiceless for the next two minutes. Then, finally she broke the silence.

"How are you?"

Her voice sounded sweet in my ears. Her luscious pecan skin and appearance looked as beautiful as I could remember.

"What do you care?" I wanted to ask.

But my heart would not allow me to be harsh towards her. I cleared my throat from the scratchiness that clung there.

"Fine and you? How have you been?" I asked as mixed feelings tortured my insides.

"I've been good. The nurse told me you just woke from your coma. That's really good."

I did not respond to her comment. She was dressed in pink sweat pants with a white tee shirt marked, "Nothing Lasts Forever, But The Love That Was Always True". I noticed her pink and white puma sneakers while she took off her matching hooded sweater and walked over to my bed. She had always been a good dresser. Right then thoughts of how much she really cared about me crossed my mind. She did not look a day in distress to me. No, I did not want her to give up on herself, but when you love someone aren't you suppose to be affected when that someone go through life threatening situations? Suddenly, resentment rose to the brim of my heart.

"Why are you here Celine?" I asked.

"Huh?"

She stood there confused and just stared at me.

"When was the last time you were here?"

"I...I don't know."

She held down her head as if she was ashamed of her truth.

"I'm sorry" she began saying.

But I quickly shut her up.

"No need to be sorry Celine, you made your decision. But, I don't understand why you would come now."

"Chris..."

"No need Celine," I bellowed annoyed, "please just leave."

I wished I had the heart to rip her the way I really wanted to. Yet, I could not because she was still Celine, the woman I wanted to spend the rest of my life with.

"Ok, if that's what you really want," she agreed.

With a disappointed expression on her face she left the room. As the door clicked shut a tear instantly fell from my eye.

Sheria

"*I can't remember* the last time I came here. I had forgotten how beautiful this place was," I said.

"I try to come by at least once a month, I'm a big fan of nature and all it's beauty."

"I would never think that a man would enjoy the botanical gardens to make a priority to come by so often."

"Well, there are a lot of things about me that some women can't appreciate," Ricky continued.

That comment gave me a bit of a scare. I hoped that he was not some sort of freak. After all, we were not acquainted to the point where I would at least guess. Besides, looks are very deceiving.

"Like what?" I was curious to know.

"Many women just want to be wined and dined and still act wild, if you know what I mean. They can't be satisfied, so it's hard for them to keep up with just one relationship. I very much believe in devotion."

"I find that reasoning hard to believe because many women I know just want to find a decent man. But, when they do find one it's a headache for them to settle down and make a commitment," I stated.

"That too. I guess some people suffer regardless. Some can't find good partners, and those who have, refuse to commit," he said.

"Yep, I think you summed it up right," I replied.

"So what about you?" he inquired.

"Right now I fit neither. I'm going through something right now and my main concern is getting over that."

There was a pause as Ricky stopped to finger the green leaves of a foreign plant. I admired his solace, wanted to break into his world and steal some of his humility.

"I was bold that night when I walked up to you. I was attracted to something about you. I'm happy I got up enough nerve to come over because I think we'll make great friends," I continued.

Surely he had caught on to my purpose. He should have understood, even though it was an indirect comment, that all I wanted was friendship. Ricky was a handsome, intelligent, and seemingly a mature man. Still, dealing with Pelvic Inflammatory Disease was enough for me right then.

"What about you?" I asked.

"I'm in neither category right now. Not looking, yet I hope to see when the right one comes along."

"And what's right for you?" I asked.

That thought came to my mind and before I got a chance to stop myself it rolled right off my tongue sending mixed signals.

"Smart, funny, adventurous because I like to travel and get to know different places and things, be fertile and willing to put it to use..."

Before Ricky could finish his comment I tripped over a large pebble and fell to the ground. I don't know which was most embarrassing; the fact that I liked him and secretly hoped for something more to develop between us or me falling on my ass in front of him.

"Are you ok?" he asked.

Ricky was at my side before I knew it, eyes filled with concern.

"Yes, thank you."

He stretched his hand and I could not refuse it. After he helped me up all I wanted to do was run away.

"Um Ricky, I have to go now. I'll call you."

Before he could reply I ran off and left him standing alone.

"Sheria wait! Wait!" he cried out after me.

But my mind was set on my destination ahead. I knew he was running after me because I heard his voice at a steady pace behind. Eventually, Ricky gave up probably wondering what kind of a nut I was running off like that. I continued running though. I sped through the gate, turned the corner, ran to my car, and drove off with so much speed that I almost knocked down a light pole. When I felt safely out of his way I pulled over and the tears flowed easily down my cheeks.

Celine

As I sank into quick sand my emotions seemed incapable of being saved. When I went back to St. Joney's three days earlier Chris had already been released. His pretend ignorance of my calls gave me the cold shoulder feeling he probably had felt when I had done the same to him. He did not care how I felt, and would not give me the chance to verbalize my thoughts or behavior towards him. I had been unsure of what I would have been greeted with when I went to visit him that day. Yet, when I left him I had felt lower than scum. I picked up my white cordless and dialed his number again.

"Hi, this is Chris. Leave me a message and I'll holla back...beep!"

I decided to try his cell.

"Your call has been forwarded to..."

I felt disappointment as I hung up the phone and resumed to my lounging. I laid in my stressing position on my bed, on my back, with my legs vertical, and feet resting on the wall. I had not thought of it before, but when Sheria brought it up, my guilt for dating Rob behind Chris's back began to swallow me up. Although it all meant nothing to me I knew that it was still wrong.

"Ring! Ring! Ring!"

I wanted to ignore the phone because I was not really in the mood to speak with anyone right then. But

I knew better to answer because she would have kept calling. Besides, I knew she was concerned about me, and perchance wanted to know about Chris' health.

"Hi mom!"

"Hey sweetie, what's going on?"

"Nothing much. I'm just laying down."

"You ok?"

Her amount of constant concern sometimes bothered me because it made me feel as though I was unable to take care of myself. Most times, however, I convinced myself that she did not mean any harm; it was just all about love.

"Yeah, I'm fine."

"How's Chris doing?"

"Good."

"Are you two still beefing?"

I had to crack a smile at my mother's choice of word. It always sounded so funny to me hearing an older person speak with the latest slangs.

"We're not beefing mom. He's just mad at me. Although I really want him to accept my apology, I can understand why he is upset right now."

"He'll come around honey, don't worry. It must have been pretty hard for him to face such tragedy alone."

"I know mom! I keep getting told."

By that time I had grown a tad annoyed.

"I sensed from the beginning that you two would develop something singular. He sounded so earnest and bona fide. I think you two will get it together, I really do."

It was becoming overbearing for me to talk about Chris any longer. My guilt continued to devour my heart and mind spiting me for having left Chris the way that I had. I had to get off the phone.

"Mom, can I call you back? I have to finish up something."

She hesitated, taken aback by my request. But like a mother always knows, she knew that I just could not deal with what I was being forced to reap. She gave in understandably.

"Ok sweetie, you take care of yourself ok? And if you need to talk call me!"

She stressed the necessity for me to call her if I needed, and I agreed with thoughts that I probably would not need to.

"Thanks mom. I will."

I placed the phone back in its cradle. My first instinct was how neglected Chris must have felt when I had disregarded him. I committed to my memory that even though I was devastatingly mad at him before, love for him still engulfed my heart. I imagined that he felt the same way for me, and that I just needed a new way to get through to him. I picked up my phone just then and decided to work with my thoughts.

"Hello?" Pete answered on the second ring.

"Hi Pete this is Celine..."

"I know, what's up?"

He sounded aggravated at the sound of my voice.

"Uhm, can you meet me in about an hour please? There's something very important I need to talk with you about."

"Can't you say on the phone?" he asked.

"No. Please, it will only take a few minutes," I insisted.

He paused again making no attempt to veil the fact that he was not fascinated by the idea of seeing or even hearing me for that matter.

"Ok, where?" he asked.

We made arrangements and that did a lot for my day. I would make Chris change his mind, I vowed to get him back.

Sheria

My blood test results came back, which confirmed my infertility.

"Shouldn't I have had some symptoms doctor?" I asked.

"Unfortunately PID is not always accompanied by obvious symptoms such as fever, abdominal pain and vaginal discharge. This is referred to as "silent" because many patients with Salpingitis recall having no symptoms at all. There are different causes of PID. A germ called Chlamidia Tracomatis, which is the most common cause of sexually transmitted diseases, caused yours."

"How come there are no other ways of finding out before the disease gets this far? Isn't it common?" I wanted to know.

"Well, it is a major health problem in the US because as many as five hundred thousand women experience an episode each year. However, because some patients have no symptoms there is no "standard" diagnostic procedure. So the disease is sometimes discovered from suspicions from your doctor during a normal check-up. Then to help confirm the presence of infection your doctor will do a couple of blood tests."

I sighed heavily while I took in all the information being thrown at me. Doctor Peterson busied himself looking for something on his huge, brown, hardwood desk top as he continued his explanation.

"Anymore questions Ms. Roberts?" he asked.

"So what's next?" I asked, very reluctant to be educated for fear.

"It is not necessary that you be admitted to the hospital so you'll be treated on an outpatient basis. I will prescribe two medications for you; Ofloxacin (also called Floxin) four hundred milligrams along with Metronadazole (also called Flagyl) five hundred milligrams. Both of these are to be taken orally twice a day for fourteen days. However, in three days you need to come back so we can check if the medications are working. If they are not working you will need to be hospitalized at that time to be treated under supervision. Also, your partner needs to be treated so that you will not re-infect each other. Please keep in mind that seventy-five percent of PID cases occur in sexually active women under twenty-five years of age. The best prevention, being that once you have it, PID could recur, is to stick with one partner or refrain from sex."

Boy was I exhausted!

"Thanks doctor."

I took my prescription and got up to leave.

"Remember you need to come back in three days, it's very important," he reminded.

"Yes, thank you."

I opened the door and barely wobbled down the hallway and out to my car. I was furious with myself to think that all this happened because of my promiscuity. I was unable to have any kids and worse I would have to be hospitalized if the medication did not work. The severity of the situation was no joke, I just wanted to get passed the beginning. My mind drifted to Ricky and how unfortunate the timing was when we met. Finally, I had visualized myself settled in a relationship. But that thought could no longer remain in my plans.

My up-curled lips showed the glee that I felt after eventually getting home and could just relax. My shoes were flung from my feet at the door. My purse landed on the firmness of my couch and remained stagnant. My clothes were peeled off, and I immediately crawled under my purple polka dotted pink comforter. Then, as usual as I drifted off to enjoy some good sleep the phone rang. I stretched over to the small stand at the side of my bed and glimpsed the caller's id. I then took up the cordless purple phone and pressed the talk button.

"'Sup girl?" I asked.

"You sound so beat."

"I am. 'Sup?" I repeated.

"Just called to tell you about my plans," Celine said.

Her excitement pulled me in.

"What plans," I asked a bit more attentively.

"For Chris. Still have feelings for him Sher and I have to try something. I really feel like this will work."

"I know you still have feelings for him. So what's the deal?" I asked.

Celine gave me the whole run-down of how she had called Pete and what she had set up with him. She was so excited and I was very happy for her.

"Aight! You go girl! sounds good to me," I encouraged.

"Thanks sis talk to you later."

"Ok bye."

I smiled because I knew to myself that there was no reason why her plan would not have worked. My comforter warmed my body once more as I snuggled beneath it and drifted off.

Chris

I was broken hearted. I could not avoid Celine's calls any longer so I decided to hang out with Pete for a while. He had been kind and gladly accommodated me in his walk-in basement apartment. He owned a laundry mat business which did pretty well. But Pete decided to rent a small place so that he would be able to save as much cash as possible. I felt comfortable chilling on his couch for the previous three days. Still, I began to feel out of place because a man needed his space, friends or no friends.

Pete, considering my interest, had insisted that I stayed longer. But I convinced him that I would have been fine. I had just gotten home and decided to run myself a bubble bath. While waiting for the tub to get full I called a Chinese restaurant located a few blocks down the street.

"Hello? Chinese Plate, may I please help you?" a female voice rung through in a Chinese accent.

"Yeah, can I have a large order of shrimp and broccoli with yellow vegetable fried rice?"

"Delivery o pick-up?"

"Delivery."

"Telephon number?"

"555-000-0000."

That will be teng dollars. Be there in thirty-five minutes," she said.

That particular take-out spot stayed hopping so usually the wait really did take twenty-five minutes or more. I had hoped that on that day the food would have taken a shorter time because I was starved.

After I made sure that my bath was nice and warm I went in my bedroom and took off my clothes. One luxury that I enjoyed from my own space was the comfort of being able to walk around in the nude. I bent down, picked up my pile of clothes from the rug, and carried them to the hamper kept in the hallway closet. Anticipating the delivery man I decided to get my payment and tip ready, then located my robe to cover myself up. Just as I put my arm in the second sleeve the bell rang. I finished tying the knot and went to the door.

"Hi," I greeted.

"Hi, teng dollars please," he responded with outstretched palm.

I handed the skinny light-skinned Chinese man eleven dollars and took my food.

"Thenk you," he said.

"Welcome, thanks."

I opened the bag and dished out most of the food on a plate, poured myself some juice and went into the bathroom. My filled glass rested at the side of the tub and my food on the toilet while I got into the tub. I finished the grub in less than no time although the food was still hot. Then when I dreamed relaxation would find me in the warm comfort of my tub full of bubbles, only disturbing thoughts followed. My mind would not leave Celine out and I could no longer control it.

I hurried out of the tub after frustrated moments of trying to think of something to get myself sleepy. I got dressed took up my car keys and some money before heading out the door. Although my destination was unknown, my purpose was clear, anything to get Celine out of my mind.

Celine

All plans were in order except for one thing. I had high hopes of everything going as thought, yet I could not simply ignore the possibility that my expectations might crumble. I had been so happy throughout my planning. But, only four hours away from the occasion, nervousness and fear overtook me wholly. I decided to call Sheria to help me to at least clear my mind.

"Hey girl," she answered after fumbling on the next line with her phone.

"What's up? You in a wrestle mania or something?" I joked.

"Nah, but my phone did try to tackle me there for a minute," she humored back.

"Oh."

"So what's up?" she asked.

"I'm feeling kinda nervous about tonight."

"Why?"

"Don't know, maybe I'm scared he'll reject me."

"He won't trust me. He'll be there," she said.

"I guess it's just the knot I have in my stomach."

"Hold on a sec. Celine."

I heard Sheria whisper something in the background before she came back on the phone.

"Sorry girl."

"Who's that?" I asked in curiosity.

"A friend of mine."

"What friend of yours?" I dug deeper.

"Let's talk later?" she asked.

I hesitated and then told her okay understanding that perhaps I had put her on the spot. I hung up the phone and tried to sneak in a nap so I would feel rested later.

Sheria

I had been walking around town with Ricky when Celine called. I excused myself for a minute because she sounded very worried. My friendship with Ricky was new and simple so I wanted to keep it on a hush-hush basis. But, Celine caught me off guard so I knew I had to divulge the details later that night.

For days after I ran off on Ricky, he rang the life out of my phone, but I blew him off, however, with my various excuses. Eventually, I agreed to meet him that day as I determined that I needed to be direct and get things over with.

"Is everything ok?" he asked with genuine concern.

"Yeah, just my best friend. She'll be fine, just nervous about something she plans to do later," I replied.

"Would you like to stop somewhere for a cup of coffee or something?" Ricky asked.

"Sure! Star Bucks is right up the block at the corner. We can stop there," I responded.

"Fine by me."

After we had settled in and received our orders I knew it was time for the inevitable.

"So Sheria, I guess I should start since I was the one who invited you here," Ricky started.

I looked at him then slowly removed my eyes from his direct stare and glued them to my cup of Espresso Roast.

He continued, "I know we've only been acquainted with each other a few days, but I like you. I hope it was not something that I said the other day that caused you to run off."

"I'm sorry about that. Was just having a difficult time," I interrupted.

"You seemed fine until you asked me what kind of women I was interested in."

My feet became wobbly, and my heart raced like Smarty Jones in the Preakness. I wanted so much to pick up and become The Runaway Bride, yet at the speed of light. But I knew I could not, knew that I had to face the music.

"Well, ah... I like you and that's the reason that nervousness overcame me. You sounded so passionate about all that you want from a relationship. It was so incredible the way your eyes sparkled when you spoke of kids... I don't know what to say really other than there can never be anything more than friendship between us."

"How can you say that when we haven't had a chance to get to know each other well enough?"

Ricky seemed reasonably confused, even showed some frustration.

"I know what you want and I know that I can never give it to you," I assured him.

"Can you just be straight with me and at least tell me what's really going on?" he asked with a heavy sigh.

At that point I could hardly hold up any longer. I looked away from him and my eyes met his tan Timberlands. My vision crawled up his black jeans pants until they passed them and went to his cream t-shirt. My eyes then held his in a trance.

"I...I can't have kids,' I stated ashamed.

Ricky paused and stared at me as though he expected my vocals to become activated again. When it became clear that I did not have anything else to say he broke the deafening silence.

"That's it?" he asked disoriented.

"What are you talking about? What do you mean if that's it?" I asked.

My confusion rung through like an old grandfather's clock.

"Just what I said. Is that all?" he insisted.

"Yeah," I gave in.

"Well, Sheria, like I said before, you did not even give us a chance to get acquainted. If you had then you would have realized that no *one* thing count to me. It takes a combination of various ingredients to make something tasty. Likewise, it takes more than a sole value or situation to make a relationship work."

His depth and passion hypnotized me.

"But you spoke so highly about children."

"Yes I did. I do love kids. If everything else is good in a relationship then I believe that alternative measures can make the circle complete."

I wanted to hug and squeeze him right then and there. The next thing I knew my elation overtook me and led to our very first kiss, and a new page turned in my life.

Chris

"Partaay!"

I stepped back from the mirror and did Carlton's dance from "The Fresh Prince of Belair". I was in my house talking to myself and getting dressed for a spectacular evening with my pal Pete. He had told me that what he had planned for me was a once in a lifetime thing. Still, Pete had not divulged any information because he deemed it a surprise. My boy always looked out for me, and the best part was that it would take my mind off Celine for the night. He had even taken me to pick out a suit. That was reason enough to believe that what came to me next would have been huge.

I put on my double-breasted gray jacket over my gray and black plaid shirt. My tie, a nice and unusual color, blended in well with my whole appearance. On top of that my Calvin Klein leather shoes spoke tunes. The vibration of my phone along with Pete's personalized ring told me that he was calling. I hurried to locate my phone and flipped it open before I pressed the "talk" button.

"Yeah?" I answered.

"You ready cuz?" Pete asked.

"No doubt."

"Ok, be there in five. You won't be driving so leave your keys."

"Aight."

Within five minutes Pete called back once more to tell me to come out front. I opened the door and wondered whether he had been that scared when he almost lost his best friend. The silver stretched limousine looked exquisite as I admired its sheen. I could hardly believe that my boy went through such lengths for me. My legs paced down the pathway to meet the well-dressed driver who opened the door for me.

"Thank you," I said to him still astonished.

The older white man closed the door after a greeting and we pulled off within the next few seconds. My eyes gazed around for Pete but I was unaccompanied. I guess he anticipated my reaction because my phone vibrated just then.

"What's up man?" I asked concerned.

"Don't worry, the driver knows where to take you..."

I interrupted, "You aren't planning to kidnap me are you bro?"

Pete laughed and so did I.

"Man, stop being a wuss," he joked.

"Hey, had to check."

"Anyway," he continued, "when you arrive just go in and give your name to the escort. He'll be expecting you."

"And then what?"

I tried to get him to spill the beans but he was not having it.

"Man just get your ass there! See you later."

The noisy dial tone rung in my ear.

My pupils began to wander as they dissected all the luxury that surrounded me. Even though I had only heard of them, this surely was one of those newly exquisite limousines. The full leather seats shined and complemented the sparkling cocktail area that announced manmade materials of sterling silver topped with crystals. Deluxe, over-the-top champagnes lined up well and boasted their expense. My mouth began to thirst for the taste of some of the Couvoursier, but I decided against it. I could not comprehend why Pete would have rented such a classic vehicle and not be there to enjoy it with me.

"What is it that he has planned?" I questioned myself.

My hands stretched and palmed the remote control that I used to turn on the fort-two inched wide screen television. I flipped through the channels and allowed my finger to paused once Pay-Per-View came in view. I leaned back and relaxed some more, then suddenly felt like I was missing something. Figuring out what it was, I was about to succumb to the temptation of the liquor when the vehicle lost motion. I sat impatiently awaiting the next move. The door flew open after a brief 'knock-knock,' so I put the remote on the seat and exited.

"This way Mr. De-Angelo."

The chauffeur closed the door behind me.

"Where's Pete and what am I doing at this restaurant? I asked with my face wrinkled with confusion.

"Your reservation is inside sir. Just go in and you will be seated."

"Is Pete inside?" I insisted.

"Sir, he is expecting you. Just go ahead inside," he stated.

I could tell that the chauffeur was becoming tried by my questions so I just went ahead and did what he suggested.

"Ok thanks."

"I'll be parked in the lot waiting sir," the bald headed man stated before he walked off to the driver's seat.

My legs took me into the Valentine's Day atmosphere of the fancy restaurant. A escort led me towards the back where the private sections were located. We stopped in front of a creme, velvet curtain decorated with pink and red flower patterns.

"Go on inside sir, your companion is expecting you."

The man walked off without giving me much time to question him. Curiosity guided my feet as they took me around the opening of the curtain. I pulled it back a tat bit. Confusion bum-rushed my brain and I became nervous. My feelings were mixed, and I felt like an invalid. I just stood there and allowed my emotions to battle it out.

A white tablecloth hugged the roundness of the table that she sat by. A picture of us together decorated its center. When I looked closer I realized that it was the same picture she kept on her dresser since the day it was developed. It held memories for me because that was the very first time that I expressed my love for her. Red rose petals laid smiling around the table's edge, on which two wrapped gift boxes stood like towers.

"Chris," she said in the softest tone.

For the first time since I saw her our eyes caressed. She hypnotized me for a moment then my eyes glided all over her. She wore her burgundy, ankle-length, spaghetti-strapped dress well. The V-neck shape of it complemented the diamond necklace that I had bought for her birthday a few months earlier. Smooth, silky skin shined, while auburn hair formed a bun to the back of her head and permitted a few sexy strands to stray. She stood and my heart pumped faster as the intoxication of her natural scent blended with White Diamonds aroused me. I froze deep in thoughts. My words refused to expel from my mouth and my limbs protested to function.

Celine

I stepped towards him. Chris stood as still as a statue except for the uncontrolled blink of his eyes. I lifted his hand and he seemed to come back to life.

"Cel..."

"Shhh!"

I stopped his thought with my manicured index finger place over his lips. He obeyed my gesture and followed as I led him to our table. I pulled out his chair and after he sat I kneeled down on a pillow facing him. I hardly knew where to begin, but I had gone that far and did not intend to turn back at that moment.

"Chris, I'm so sorry."

I paused to allow my apology to sink in.

"I was scared of losing you and devastated at the same time about your affair. Eventually, I figured I should just let you go and move on. I never meant to leave you by yourself. I was frustrated because I really loved you and thought you were different. I could not accept that you were the one to hurt me. Never in a million years I wanted to see that. But you did Chris, you blundered my heart."

Tears formed in Chris's eyes, but he did not look away.

"I'm sorry my sweet. I never meant to hurt you, please believe that if nothing else. And accept that I *am* different because I am. All that happened was a simple mistake, a simple mistake with big consequences. I don't want to lose you Celine, I need you in my life."

I could no longer hold them and so tears of relief streamed down my cheeks and lifted some stress from my shoulders. Chris lifted me up and stood with me. His arms found my shoulders and hugged me in his warmth. I, in turn, flung my arms around him and cried on his chest. We embrace for what seemed like eternity until my tears finally subsided.

"Chris?"

"Yeah?" he answered.

"I don't know what's next, but I know that I cannot deal with another mistake."

"You won't have to baby, I promise."

"How can I be sure, Chris? You destroyed the trust that was built between us."

His voice became cracked and insecurity was apparent.

"Don't know Celine, but I'm willing to do anything. I'll give you time if you want."

"I don't know yet, I'm still unsure of where we go next. I thought I was ready to move on with you, still I guess it's not that simple."

My plan had deviated from what I originally wanted to take place. I was not so sure anymore if staying together would have been the best thing for us. I stepped away from Chris and went to sit. He sat too and an uncomfortable moment danced in the air. Dinner was served and minds left to wonder about what would behold the rest of the night and the rest of 'us'.

Sheria

My treatment for PID had gone well. Yet, that did not kill my bummed out emotions caused by me being barren. I realized that sleeping around had been just an excuse for me to alleviate some of the pain that I felt from being alone. I suffered after my father's death and even more from my mother's inability to deal with it. And that led to her abandoning of me. I decided to seek counseling to help me to get over my emotional build-up of anger and to find healthy ways to cope.

It turned out that perhaps Ricky and I were supposed to meet at the time that we did, contrary to my previous belief. He proved to be such a patient and understanding man. Although, no commitment was made between us for anything more than friendship, we began to hang out more often. I really enjoyed his company and we both still liked each other very much. However, Ricky knew that I first had to heal myself before I could be in any stable relationship. We were unsure of where we were going, but for then we enjoyed what we could of each other's company.

Chris

    Celine and I remained on good terms and that was the most important thing for me. While I wished that she and I were together again, I understood the strained effect of my disloyalty. Celine decided that although she thought she was ready to move on she really was not. Therefore, she asked me to give her some time.

    My bookstores were both doing well as were all other things in my life. Yet, it remained so unbelievable that with all that I had, I still was not happy. The one thing that I wanted more than anything else could not be outweighed by all that I had.

    That Saturday morning had made two weeks since Celine and I last saw each other. I laid on my couch deep in thoughts when my bell rang. At first I was hesitant, but then I got up to answer it. I looked through the peek hole and my eyes widened. I opened the door.

    "Hey Chris," she said.

    "Hey yourself, what are you doing here?" I asked.

    "Can I come in for a few?" she asked.

    "Sure."

    I stepped aside and gave her enough room to get in. I gestured towards the couch.

    "You can have a seat if you'd like. Want something to drink?" I asked.

    "No thanks."

    Brenda was dressed much more conservative than her normal. She wore tight leather pants with a matching vest that did not broadcast much of her boobs. Her black heels clinked against the small portion of my parquet floor and then sank into the rug once she reached the living room. She sat, and I took residence in an armchair opposite her.

"Chris I came by to let you know that I'm leaving, I need a new start. Just wanted you to know that I am sorry that I tried to betray and set you up."

Her sincerity was genuine and I felt sympathy for her.

"It was not your fault Brenda, Rob brainwashed you and took advantage. I understand that you were threatened and forced to protect yourself and the safety of your son."

"I know, but I cannot put all the blame on Rob. I need to take responsibility for my own actions. I could have forced Rob to stop his evil because I knew what he was up to, but I didn't."

"Don't pressure yourself, it's all over now. Besides, like I said before I understand that you were scared."

"I was, but still that's no excuse."

Silence froze us before it let us free once more. I hugged Brenda and we said our goodbyes. She was not an evil person, in fact she had a great personality. Sometimes life just got the better of people, and sometimes we get caught in irregular situation. How was she to know anyway that Rob had psychological problems. His infatuation with Celine was also serious and I wished that it had not gotten as far as things did. Now Brenda had to face her own reality. She had ran off on me with Rob, yet in the end she was alone. My only regret was sleeping with Brenda and jeopardizing my relationship with Celine.

Epilogue (six months later)

Sheria

Four o'clock came and I was all ready to go through the door. I felt pretty hot and so I dressed accordingly. I wore a long jean skirt curved to the shape of my hips and ass. The slit that was on the front right hand side revealed as the saying goes, 'all that my mamma gave me', as all I wore underneath was a pair of skimpy red thongs that peeked over at the top of my skirt. My brown strapped up heels was the perfect combination along with the cut off shirt that revealed my belly piercing. I sprayed on some Jadore, grabbed my pocketbook, my keys and headed towards my car.

On my way over I could not jerk the thought that told me it was time to give in to my emotional sea of love. I knew that I had to begin somewhere and I believed that that was the time to just take a chance. Pumped by my energized feelings, I decided to get Ricky a special gift on my way over there. As I turned on Miller Avenue I saw a big commotion where cops surrounded about five guys. I quickly drove by not wanting to get caught in the middle just in case things got ugly. It occurred to me just how short life really could be. So I felt I had all the more reasons to act on my emotions.

A couple of miles later I stood nervously in front of his door. My heart battered my chest as if it had been held captive and was trying to free itself. My right palm raised, and as if done unconsciously, brushed back my hair to make sure that every straw was in place and then did the exact thing to my clothes. I pushed the minute white button to alert him of my arrival. Two minutes later Ricky came to the door. At that moment, he was the sexiest sight that I had ever behold.

"Hi!" I purred.

"Hi sweetie," he said.

Over the months, 'sweetie' had been Ricky's special name for me. Yet, at that instant I felt as though I had never heard it before because the sound of it electrified me. As I stepped inside I knew that after we consummated our love that night, I would step back out feeling good about myself and what we did.

Celine

"I do."

Chris stood before me in a white armani suit complemented by white shoes. His hair was braided back in a criss-crossed style and tucked under in the back. Happy rays beamed all over him as he faced me. My eyes united with his and tears formed instantly because I was glad that our day was made possible.

I memorized all that we had been through. It had been difficult for us to get passed our past, but love kept us strong. Enjoyment filled me as I stood next to the man that I loved with my best friend at my side.
Sheria took a napkin and performed her maid of honor's duty by dabbing the tears away. I glimpsed over at the crowd and saw my proud parents unable to control their glee. I blew them both a kiss and then turned back to my lover- soon to be husband.

Chris took my hand and repeated after the pastor as he placed the one-karat diamond ring on my finger. He caressed my finger so sweetly, which sent the warmest shiver through me. I glistened and mouthed, "I love you," to him and he blew me a kiss. The ceremony concluded with our jump over a broomstick to portray new beginnings. Chris and I waltzed down the isle to "Endless Love" and then boarded our chariot.

We arrived at te reception parlor in less than twenty minutes. Chris and I entered to loud cheers as everyone greeted us as Mr. And Mrs. Chris De-Angelo. I had allowed Chris to take care of our reception and must say that I was very pleased with his level of effort and success. First of all, the restaurant had become a treasured place to us and so the fact that our reception took place there was awesome. The way Chris had the place decorated was even more breathtaking. The theme colors were lavender and half-white. There were candles laid out on each of the fifteen six placed round tables. Even the hired staff wore half-white suits with lavender tunics.

I was truly happy and had no doubt in my mind that what was in store for Chris and I was long awaited. We basked in the attention, as we loved each other in the presence of friends, and families throughout the rest of the evening.

Questions for Book Club Discussions

1. What are your thoughts on how the relationship began between Chris and Celine? Did they really love each other?

2. Do you think that Sheria have gotten over her ways of promiscuity?

3. Should Celine and Chris have married in the end? Do you think their love is lasting?

4. What are your thoughts of Brenda? Do you think she is a cruel person, or do you understand why she did what she had to?

5. Was Celine wrong for turning to Rob? Did Chris push her in that direction?

6. Do you think Chris was really sorry for sleeping with Brenda?

Acknowledgments

I would like to first of all thank God, who wakes me and keeps me each day.

Thanks to my sister Kay, who was the first one to read my manuscript. Mom, thanks for all your guidance throughout the years. I love you both. Gennell, keep your head up, and remember that you can be anything that you want to be. Just believe and never give up!

Romeric, you have been there with me each step of the way. Thanks for the support and extra help when I needed it most. It's finally over (at least the beginning), and Gary doesn't have to be baffled anymore:) Love you!

Special thanks to Kerwin, who continues to be an inspiration to many, including myself. Thanks for all your support. Fernando, I appreciate your answers to my million and one computer questions.

Thanks to the moderators and members of BWunited, RI C, Review and Authors, and Blackexpressions2005 online yahoo groups for your welcome and support.

Tim Sheard (author of "Some Cuts Never Heal" and "The Fire in My Soul: a memoir with Delbert McCoy"), Loretta Campbell and all who contributed to the workshops with the National Writers Union, as well as DC37 union, I am grateful for the valuable information that have been imparted to me.

Much love and appreciation to my BPL family for their continued support. Candice and Terry, you are such good friends to have.

I also want to thank everyone who have supported me along the way. I appreciate you all.

Until next time...keep reading and be on the look out for my upcoming novel:)

About The Author

Nicola McDonald has always been fond of writing. Ever since she remembers herself being able to write she has enjoyed, and cherished her capabilities of writing, and using her imagination so creatively. Two years ago she decided to take the craft that she loves to another level, to see her dream of becoming a published writer come true.

Along with novels, Nicola also writes poems and short stories. Her poetry was published in an anthology earlier this year. She enjoys modeling, listening to music, and also prides herself on being an avid reader. She is an active member of various online reading groups, as well as offline book clubs.

Nicola works at a public library in New York and lives in the Bronx. She is currently working on her next novel.

Nicola would love to hear from you! Visit her website at www.newnpublishing.com for more info or email her directly at n_mcd@msn.com